W9-BLU-051

"In order to protect baby Angelina, I need a wife—you have said so yourself. Under the circumstances, who better to be that wife than you?"

"What?" Alice was gripped by shock. "No," she whispered. "We can't. I can't."

"Yes, we can. We have to," Marco insisted fiercely. "For Angelina's sake."

Here was a man who was totally dedicated to protecting the child fate had placed in his care, even to the extent of marrying a woman he did not love, in order to do so. She loved Angelina, too—could she do any less?

"So far as you and I are concerned, it will simply be a business arrangement," he told her calmly.

How could she agree to a business arrangement of a marriage with Marco when she loved and wanted him so much? Hadn't this afternoon taught her anything at all?

"Yes!" That he was the most wonderful man to be kissed by, she found herself thinking recklessly.

Legally wed,
But he's never said…
"I love you."

They're…

The series where marriages are made in
haste…and love comes later….

This month we bring you
Marco's Convenient Bride
by
Penny Jordan

Look out for more Wedlocked! marriage stories
in Harlequin Presents® throughout 2003.

Coming next month
Husband by Arrangement #2323
by
Sara Wood

Penny Jordan

MARCO'S CONVENIENT WIFE

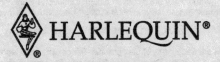

TORONTO • NEW YORK • LONDON
AMSTERDAM • PARIS • SYDNEY • HAMBURG
STOCKHOLM • ATHENS • TOKYO • MILAN • MADRID
PRAGUE • WARSAW • BUDAPEST • AUCKLAND

If you purchased this book without a cover you should be aware
that this book is stolen property. It was reported as "unsold and
destroyed" to the publisher, and neither the author nor the
publisher has received any payment for this "stripped book."

ISBN 0-373-12314-0

MARCO'S CONVENIENT WIFE

First North American Publication 2003.

Copyright © 2002 by Penny Jordan.

All rights reserved. Except for use in any review, the reproduction or
utilization of this work in whole or in part in any form by any electronic,
mechanical or other means, now known or hereafter invented, including
xerography, photocopying and recording, or in any information storage
or retrieval system, is forbidden without the written permission of the
publisher, Harlequin Enterprises Limited, 225 Duncan Mill Road,
Don Mills, Ontario, Canada M3B 3K9.

All characters in this book have no existence outside the imagination of the
author and have no relation whatsoever to anyone bearing the same
name or names. They are not even distantly inspired by any individual
known or unknown to the author, and all incidents are pure invention.

This edition published by arrangement with Harlequin Books S.A.

® and TM are trademarks of the publisher. Trademarks indicated with
® are registered in the United States Patent and Trademark Office, the
Canadian Trade Marks Office and in other countries.

Visit us at www.eHarlequin.com

Printed in U.S.A.

PROLOGUE

'GOOD luck with your interview. You're bound to get the job, though—no one could find a better nanny than you, Alice. Your only fault is that you love children too much!'

As she returned her elder sister's warm hug Alice tried to smile. Even though it was over a month since she had left her previous job she still missed her two young charges. She did not, however, miss their father, who had made her last few months in the employ of his wife so uncomfortable, with his sexual come-ons towards her.

Even without his unwanted attentions, Alice knew she would not have accepted his wife's invitation to work for them in New York, where she had been relocated.

Her former employer was in many ways typical of some career women, who whilst needing to employ a nanny to look after their children, often resented and even deliberately undermined their nanny's role within the household.

But that was the price one paid for the job she had chosen to do, and now she was about to fly to Florence to be interviewed for a new post, that of looking after a very young baby—a motherless six-month-old baby.

'And thanks for agreeing to take Louise with you,' her sister, Connie, was saying. 'I know she's going to love Florence, especially with her artistic talents. Life hasn't been very easy for her lately, so I'm hoping that this trip will help her.'

Privately Alice felt that Louise, her sister's stepdaughter, was determined to express her own misery and insecurity by making her new stepmother, Connie, and her father feel guilty about their marriage, and that she was determined that nothing they did was going to please her and that included the gift of a four-day trip to Florence. Alice had agreed to accompany her by flying out to Italy four days ahead of her interview with the awesomely patrician-sounding Conte di Vincenti, who had advertised for an Italian-speaking English nanny for 'a six-month-old child'.

It had been that 'a six-month-old child' that had not just caught Alice's eye, but more importantly had tugged at her all too vulnerable heartstrings. It had sounded so cold and distancing, as though somehow the imperious *conte* was devoid of any kind of emotional attachment to the baby, and that had immediately aroused all Alice's considerable protective instincts.

After children, languages were her second love; she was fluent in not just Italian but French and German as well—a considerable advantage in a nanny, as her agency had approvingly told her.

The last time she had visited Florence had been when she had been eight and her elder sister fifteen and she had very happy memories of that trip, so why was she feeling so apprehensive at the thought of going back?

Because she would be accompanying and be responsible for Louise, who was currently manifesting almost all of the traits of teenagedom that made her parents despair, or because there was something about the very sound of her potential new employer that sent a cold little trickle of atavistic antipathy down her spine?

Alice didn't know, but what she did know was that over and above her own feelings were the needs of a motherless six-month-old baby.

CHAPTER ONE

FLORENCE was having a heatwave and the weather was even hotter than Alice had been prepared for. Whilst Louise slept in her hotel bed, bad-temperedly refusing to join her, Alice had taken advantage of her solitude to explore the early morning city on her own. Having just seen an elegantly dressed young mother emerging from a shop with her children, all triumphantly carrying tubs of ice cream, Alice couldn't resist the temptation of indulging in the same treat herself.

After all, according to her guidebook Florence was famous for its ice cream.

Carefully she started to make her way across the busy street, not really paying much attention to the vehicle that was blocking the road, although she was aware of a bright red and very expensive-looking sports car that was bearing down on both her and the parked vehicle. Just beyond her, the street ended in a set of lights, and as they were on red she determinedly chose to ignore the angry blare of the car's horn.

However, she was conscious of its delayed and engine throbbing presence behind her at the traffic lights as she gave and received her order for a tiramisu ice cream—her favourite Italian sweet. The young male assistant serving her made a boldly flirtatious comment as he handed her her change—bold enough to make her face flush bright pink, and loud enough, she realised as she turned away, for the man behind the wheel of the scarlet open-topped mechanical monster still waiting for both the obstruction to be moved and the lights to change, to have heard.

To have heard and to be thoroughly contemptuous of,

she recognised as she saw the way he looked down the length of his aquiline nose at her, his mouth curling in open disdain.

Totally mortified, Alice could feel her face burning even hotter, her enjoyment of her ice cream completely destroyed by her recognition of his contempt of her. No doubt he thought she was some silly Northern European tourist looking for a cheap holiday fling, she fumed as she gave him a look intended to be as corrosive as the one he had just given her. Unfortunately, though, she had not allowed for the effect of the extremely hot sun on her ice cream and as she turned to glower at him, in what she had planned to be a rebuffing and ladylike manner, she realised that her ice was dripping onto her top.

And that of course was the reason why her nipples should suddenly choose that totally inauspicious moment to peak openly and flauntingly with maddening wilfulness. And all the while she had to stand there waiting to cross the road, with his gaze pinned with deliberate emphasis and insulting thoroughness on the swell of her breasts.

Horrible, horrid man, she designated him under her breath, but she knew as she did so that he was also just about the most sensually magnetic and dangerous man she had ever set eyes on.

Just the merest link between her own bemused, shocked eyes and the hooded, mesmeric topaz intensity of his would have been enough to melt a full glacier, never mind her ice cream, she reflected shakily once he had driven past her.

And that was without him trying. Heaven alone knew what he could do if he really tried to turn a deliberately sensual look on a woman! Not that she was ever likely to know or want to know. Of course not! No. Never. Definitely not!

And as for that open-topped car—in this heat—well, that was obviously a deliberate pose, meant to underline his macho masculinity. She despised men like that! Men who needed to reinforce their machismo. Not that he had looked as though his needed much reinforcing—and no doubt that thick head of dark, dark brown but not quite jet-black hair would ensure that his scalp would never need protecting from strong sunlight.

'Damn the woman, where is she?' Marco looked irritably at his watch, and then frowned as he studied the empty foyer of the exclusive and expensive hotel just outside Florence, where he had arranged to meet the English-woman he was supposed to be interviewing. He was stalk-ing imperiously up and down its imposing length with a lean and predatory male animal stride that caused the fe-male hotel guest crossing the foyer to give a small, un-stoppable little hormonal shiver of appreciation.

Oblivious of his effect on her, Marco continued to frown.

The fact that his interviewee had neither the discipline to be on time for their meeting, nor the good manners to send a message apologising for her late appearance, was not in his opinion a good advertisement for her profes-sional skills, despite the fact that she had come so highly recommended by her agency that it had virtually sung a paean of praise in her favour.

He had not been in the best of moods even before he'd reached the city. His car, the normally totally reliable sa-loon he drove, had developed some kind of electrical prob-lem, which meant that it was currently being repaired, leaving him with no alternative but to drive the ridiculous and, to his mind, totally over the top bright red Ferrari, which had belonged to his cousin Aldo, but which since Aldo's death had remained at the *palazzo*.

Unlike his Mercedes, the Ferrari was certainly the kind of car that attracted a good deal of attention—and the wrong kind of attention in Marco's opinion. His eyes nar-rowed slightly as he remembered the blonde girl he had noticed when he had driven into the city earlier in the day on his way to meet a colleague.

Her body had certainly approved of the car, even if her eyes had flashed him a look of murderous, 'don't you dare look at me like that' rejection, he reflected wryly.

Personally, he would far rather have a woman be attracted to him for himself than his car! Aldo, though, had not shared his feelings!

Where was this wretched girl?

To be truthful it had irked him a little that she had refused to stay in this hotel as he had wished. Instead she'd insisted on staying, albeit at her own expense, in a far less convenient, so far as he was concerned, hotel in the centre of Florence itself. This was apparently because she wished to do some sightseeing and because she had been concerned that the hotel he had chosen was too far out of the city centre and too quiet. An ominous statement, so far as Marco was concerned! As a student at university in England, he had witnessed the way in which some English girls chose to demonstrate their dislike of anything 'too quiet'!

Perhaps it was old-fashioned of him to abhor promiscuity, and to believe that a person—of either sex—should have enough self-restraint and enough self-pride not to treat sex as an emotionless act of physical gratification on a par with eating a bar of chocolate, but that was how he felt.

Irritably he shot back the cuff of his immaculately tailored pale grey suit and frowned. Angelina, the baby for whom he was seeking the services of a nanny, would be awake and wondering where he was. The traumatic loss of her mother had left the baby clinging to the only other adult who was a constant in her life, and who she seemed to feel safe with, and that was himself. Marco was not impressed with the standard of care or commitment the girl who'd originally been hired by Angelina's late mother was currently giving to the baby.

Grimly Marco reminded himself that now Angelina was his child, and that she was totally dependent on him in every single way. Right now it was Angelina who needed to come first in his thoughts and his actions. That was why he was so determined not to find merely 'a nanny' for her, but the right nanny, the best nanny—a nanny who would be prepared to commit herself, her time and to some extent her future to being with Angelina.

And this was where a battle was being fought inside him. His frown changed from that of irritated, almost antagonistic male, to one of deeply concerned protective paternalism. He felt such a strong sense of family and emotional responsibility to Angelina, that the only woman he would entrust the baby with had to be someone who could supply her with the love and security her mother's death had deprived her of, someone warm and loving, reliable and responsible.

And as the baby's mother had been British, he had decided to advertise for an Italian speaking British nanny for Angelina, so that she would grow up learning both languages.

The girl he had eventually settled on had in many ways almost seemed to be too good to be true, she had been so highly recommended and praised by her agency. But then of course they would not necessarily be dispassionate about her!

Now it seemed that he had been right to be dubious. Grimly he rechecked his watch. His autocratic features were so arrogantly and blatantly those of a sensually mature adult Italian male that it was no wonder the pretty girl behind the reception desk was watching him with awed longing.

He positively exuded power and masculinity, laced with a dangerous hint of potent sexuality. Just as the lean animal grace of the way he walked failed to cloak that maleness, so too the elegant tailoring failed to cloak the fact that the body beneath it was all raw magnificence and muscle. He possessed that kind of bred-into-the-bone sensuality that no woman could fail to recognise and respond to, be it with longing or apprehension. The kind of sensuality that went much, much deeper than the mere good looks with which nature had so generously endowed him, the kind of sensuality that neither money nor power nor position could buy!

There was, though, a touch of grim determination about the hard line of his mouth that set him apart from most other men of his race, a certain cool hauteur and distance that challenged anyone who dared to come too close to him uninvited.

At thirty-five he had behind him over a decade of heading the vast and complicated tangled network of his extended family; aunts, uncles, and cousins.

His father and mother had been killed outright when his father's younger brother had crashed the private plane he had been flying. Marco, or, to give him his correct name, Semperius Marco Francisco Conte di Vincenti, had been twenty-five at the time, and freshly qualified as an architect, aware of the responsibility of the role that would ultimately be his, the guardian of his family's history and the guardian too of its future, but relieved to know that that responsibility would not truly be his for many years to come. And then his father's unexpected death had thrown him head first into shouldering what had then seemed to be an extraordinarily heavy burden.

But somehow he had carried it—because it had been his duty to do so, and if in doing so he had lost some of the spontaneity, the love of life and laughter and the ability to live for the moment alone that had so marked out his younger cousin, Aldo, like him left fatherless by the crash, then those around him had just had to accept that that had been so.

Some of the older members of the family considered that he had allowed Aldo to take advantage of him, he knew. But like him his cousin had lost his father in the tragedy, and, at only sixteen, it surely must have been a far harder burden for him to bear than it had been for Marco himself.

Marco's frown deepened as he thought about his younger cousin. He had been totally opposed to Aldo marrying Patti, the pretty English model. The wedding had taken place within weeks of Aldo meeting her, and it had not surprised him in the least to learn that they had fallen out of love with one another as quickly as they had fallen into it.

But there was no point in dwelling on that now. Aldo had married Patti, and baby Angelina had been conceived, even if both her parents had by that time been claiming that their marriage had been a mistake and that they bitterly regretted the legal commitment they had made to one another.

It had been in his role of head of the family that Marco had felt obliged to invite them both to visit them at his home in Tuscany, in the hope that he could somehow help them to find a way of making their marriage work. After all, whilst he might not have approved of it in the first place, they now had a child to consider, and in Marco's eyes the needs of their child far outweighed the selfish carnal desires of either of her parents.

But, once he had left them to their own devices, an argument had broken out between Aldo and Patti, which had resulted in Aldo driving Patti away from the villa in a furious temper.

They would probably never know just what had caused the fatal accident, which had claimed their lives and left their baby an orphan, Marco reflected sombrely, but he knew just how responsible he felt for having been the one to have brought them both to the *palazzo* in the first place.

As Aldo's next of kin he had naturally taken on full responsibility for the orphaned baby, and now three months later it was abundantly obvious that little Angelina had bonded strongly with Marco. Marco's strong paternalistic instincts had meant that he had decided that it was both his duty and in the baby's own interests for him to make proper arrangements for her care.

In order to cut down on wasting time unnecessarily on interviews that would not lead anywhere, he had painstakingly spent far more time than he could currently afford sifting through the applications he had received, to make sure that he only interviewed the candidate or candidates who met all his strict criteria, and in the end Alice Walsingham had been the only one to do so; which made it even more infuriating that she had not even taken the trouble to turn up for their interview. It was eleven o'clock, half an hour past the time of their appointment. His patience finally snapped. That was it! He had waited long enough. If Miss Walsingham did ever decide to turn up, she was most definitely not the person he wanted to leave in sole charge of his precious child. Not even to himself was Marco prepared to admit just how attached he had become to his cousin's baby, or how paternal he felt towards her.

As he stepped out of the hotel into the bright Florentine sunshine it glinted on the darkness of his thick, well-groomed hair, highlighting his chiselled, autocratic features, and the lean-muscled strength of his six-foot-two frame.

Automatically he shielded the fierceness of his topaz gaze from the harshness of the sun by putting on dark glasses that gave him a breath-catching air of predatory power and danger.

An actor studying for a role as a Mafiosi leader would have found him an ideal model. He looked lean, mean and dangerous. No one would dream of making a man who looked as he did any kind of offer he might be tempted to refuse!

Irritably he returned to where he had left Aldo's Ferrari, which was parked outside the hotel, and he had just climbed into it and put the keys in the ignition when he suddenly remembered that he had not left any message for his dilatory interviewee, just in case she should choose to turn up!

Leaving the keys in the ignition, he climbed out of the Ferrari and strode toward the hotel.

'Oh, for God's sake, will you stop nagging me? You aren't my mother, you aren't anything to me. Just because your sister has managed to trap my father into marriage that doesn't give you the right to tell me what to do.'

As she listened to Louise's deliberately hostile and inflammatory speech Alice mentally counted to ten.

It was now five minutes past eleven, and she was over half an hour late for her interview appointment, but it had been impossible for her to leave Louise to her own devices after the teenager's totally unacceptable behaviour during their trip.

The previous night, Louise had sneaked out of the hotel without her, returning in the early hours very much the worse for drink, refusing to tell Alice where she had been or who with. Alice had been beside herself with anxiety.

As luck would have it, Alice had now learned that her sister's stepdaughter had spent the evening with a group of young American students who were studying in the city, and who it seemed had thankfully kept a watchful eye on her whilst she had been with them.

However, as one of the students had a little anxiously explained to Alice, Louise had spent a large part of the evening in conversation with a rather unsavoury character who had attached himself to the group and now it seemed Louise had made arrangements to meet up with the man.

In order to ensure that she did not do so, Alice had insisted that Louise accompany her to her interview.

Forced to do so, Louise had left Alice in no doubt about her feelings of resentment and hostility, as well as deliberately making Alice late for her appointment, but now, thank goodness, they had finally reached the hotel. She paid off their taxi driver, primly ignoring the appreciative look he was giving them both—two slender, blonde English beauties. One of whom, with her face plastered with far too much make-up, looked far older than her seventeen years and the other, whose clear, soft skin was virtually free of any trace of cosmetics at all, her hair a natural, soft pale blonde unlike her charge's rebelliously dyed and streaked tousled mane, looked far, far younger than her much more mature twenty-six.

Although she herself was unaware of it, even the simple skirt and top outfit she had chosen to wear for the heat of the Florentine sunshine made Alice look young enough to be a teenager herself, whilst Louise's tight jeans and midriff-baring top were drawing the interested gaze of every red-blooded Italian male who saw them.

Sulkily Louise affected not to hear what Alice was saying as she urged her to hurry into the hotel.

Under other circumstances Alice knew that she would have enjoyed simply standing to gaze in admiration at her surroundings. According to her guidebook, this particular hotel, once the home of a Renaissance prince, had been converted into a hotel with such sensitivity and skill by the architect in charge of its conversion that to stay in it was a privilege all in itself.

Unable to resist pausing simply to fill her senses with its symmetry and beauty, Alice was only aware that Louise's attention was otherwise engaged when she heard her charge exclaiming excitedly.

'Wow, just look at that car! What I'd give to be able to drive something like that.'

Turning her head, Alice was startled to see parked there in front of them an open-topped scarlet sports car like the one she had seen earlier that morning. Like, or the same? Driven by that same darkly, dangerously, and wholly male man who had looked at her as though…as though… Dragging her thoughts away from such risky and uncomfortably self-illuminating channels, Alice realised with shock that Louise was darting across towards the driver's door of the car.

'Louise,' she cautioned her anxiously. 'Don't...'

But it was too late. Totally ignoring her objections, Louise was sliding into the driver's seat, telling her triumphantly, 'The keys are in it. I've always wanted to drive a car like this...'

To Alice's horror Louise was pulling open the obviously unlocked driver's door and sliding into the driving seat. Totally appalled, Alice protested in disbelief, 'Louise, no!' unable to accept that Louise could behave so irresponsibly. 'You mustn't! You can't...'

'Who says I can't?' Louise was challenging her as she turned the key in the ignition and Alice heard the engine roar into life.

She could see a look in Louise's eyes that was completely unmistakable and her heart missed a beat. Her sister had warned her that Louise could be headstrong, and that the trauma of the break-up of her parents' marriage had affected her badly, as had the fact that her mother's new husband had made no secret that he did not want an obstreperous teenage stepdaughter on the scene to cause him problems.

Even so!

'Louise, no,' Alice protested, pleadingly, instinctively hurrying round to the passenger door of the car and wrenching it open, not really knowing what she could do, just knowing that somehow she had to stop her charge from what she was doing. But before she could do anything Louise had put the car in gear and it was starting to move, the movement jolting Alice forward.

Somehow she found that she was in the passenger seat of the car, frantically wrestling to close the door as the car set off lurchingly toward the hotel's exit.

Her heart in her mouth, Alice pleaded with Louise to stop the car, but everything she said only seemed to goad the younger girl on. Alice could hear the gears crashing as

Louise manoeuvred the car clumsily onto the road. She had only just passed her driving test, and so far had only been allowed to drive her father's sedate saloon car under his strict supervision. Alice, who could drive herself and who had driven considerable distances with her former young charges, knew that she would never have had the confidence or the skill to drive a vehicle such as this.

She gasped in shock as Louise started to accelerate, and only just missed hitting a pair of scooters bent on overtaking them.

The road stretched ahead of them, unusually straight for an Italian road, and heavy with traffic, a wall, beyond which lay the river, on one side of it and a row of four-or-so-storey buildings and a narrow pavement full of shoppers on the other.

Alice felt sick and desperately afraid, but somehow she managed to quell her instinctive urge to wrest the steering wheel from Louise's obviously inexpert grip.

Up ahead of them she could see a car pull out to overtake; she cried out a warning to Louise but, instead of slowing down, the younger girl increased her speed.

Alice held her breath, tensing her body against the collision, which she knew to be inevitable.

CHAPTER TWO

IT WAS the unmistakable sound of Aldo's Ferrari's engine being inexpertly fired that first alerted Marco to what was going on.

Sprinting towards the main road, he reached it just in time to see the two blonde heads of the female thieves who had stolen the car, which was now being driven with teeth-clenching lack of expertise towards the Tuscan countryside.

However, it wasn't the lack of driving expertise they were displaying that brought a grim look of tension to Marco's mouth. No, what was concerning him was the fact that he feared an accident, and, having already lost a much-loved cousin as well as having had to identify both his and the destroyed body of what had originally been a very pretty young woman, he had no wish to see history repeating itself.

He was already reaching for his mobile to report the theft when he heard and saw the collision he had been dreading.

To his relief he realised immediately that the crash was not a serious one. The driver of the other car was already out of his vehicle and heading for the Ferrari, which Marco could see had barely been damaged by the impact at all.

Cancelling the call, he started to run towards the scene.

Above the sound of Louise's frantic screams, Alice could hear the sound of approaching Italian voices. Her head ached where she had banged it on the windscreen, and as she tried to blink the pain away she realised that Louise was already standing on the pavement, beside the car, whilst somehow she herself was lying across both seats, with her head now against the driver's headrest.

She knew she had to get out of the car. And she knew the easiest way to do that would be to slide her legs over to the driver's side of the car, but her thoughts would only assemble in slow and painful motion as they fought their way through the dizzying sickness of her shock.

Someone, predictably a man, was comforting Louise, who was crying hysterically, but no one, Alice noticed, was bothering to help her. Somehow, though, she managed to get herself out of the car, just as the crowd that was surrounding it parted to allow through the tall, dark-haired and even darker-browed man who was now talking with the driver of the car they'd crashed into, handing him his card.

Then as he turned to look at her she recognised him. Alice thought she was going to faint. She would have recognised that eagle-eyed, imperious topaz stare anywhere, and she could tell from the way his glance moved from her face down to her breasts that he remembered exactly who she was as well.

It was the man she had seen earlier that morning, the man who…. Her head was throbbing and instinctively Alice pressed her hand to her temple. She felt so dizzy and sick, so unable somehow to draw her own gaze away from that angry, burning hostility of pure male fury. The shock of what had happened seemed to have robbed her of her normal self-control and maturity. Feeling as though she was going to cry, she longed desperately to have someone to turn to, some sturdy, reliable, pro-Alice male presence there to support and protect her. Such unfamiliar and undermining thoughts increased her sense of alienation from her normal 'self'.

He of the angry eyes and hard, forbidding mouth was focusing on her so intently that she felt like a helpless specimen trapped beneath a microscope.

In the distance Alice could hear Louise sobbing frantically, 'It wasn't my fault. I didn't do anything. She was the one who was driving the car. Not me...'

But although she registered what Louise was saying it barely made any impact on her at all. And the reason for that was the man now standing in front of her, towering over her, all six-foot odd, furiously cold, dangerously angry and intensely male of him, addressing her in icily perfect and whiplash sharp English as he demanded, 'If you are the perpetrator of this...this atrocity, then let me tell you now I fully intend to see that you pay for it. Have you any idea what you have done? The danger...the risk... someone could have been killed.' His voice became acidly sharp and harsh. 'Have you ever seen a victim of a serious road accident? Do you have any idea what it can do to the human body?'

Fresh nausea overwhelmed Alice. He wasn't saying anything to her she hadn't already thought for herself, but Louise, who could hear him, was now silent and ashen-faced, and instinctively Alice felt her first duty was to protect her. And now that she could see both cars, she could see too that surely he was overreacting. Anxiously she looked towards his car. The passenger door was crushed, there was broken glass all over the road. The car they had hit had lost its bumper and sustained a large dent, although fortunately its driver seemed to be unhurt, and indeed he was very evidently comforting Louise, who was shaking uncontrollably, telling everyone who would listen to her that it had been Alice who had been driving the car and not her.

Alice opened her mouth to correct her and defend herself and then closed it again.

How could she? Louise was seventeen; she had only just passed her driving test. Last night she had been drinking so heavily that she probably still had a dangerously high level of alcohol in her bloodstream, and she was in Alice's charge... Alice had promised her sister that she would take care of her...

Unaware of what she was doing, she looked up at the man confronting her in helpless appeal.

Marco felt himself stiffen as he saw the look Alice was giving him. She looked more like a child than a woman, with the pale swathe of her cheeks and her huge bruised eyes and trembling mouth; her delicately slender body. But he of course already knew about the sensuality and the voluptuousness of the breasts that were now concealed by a much bulkier top than the little strappy one she had been wearing earlier in the day when he had seen her.

Disconcertingly and with unexpected force his body responded to that memory and to her. Immediately Marco quelled his swift surge of unwanted physical reaction, waiting for what he already knew she was going to say to him, the appeal she was going to make to him, on behalf of herself and her companion.

He had seen beautiful women using their beauty to get what they wanted so many many times before. And of course the first thing this beautiful woman was going to do was to tell him what he had already worked out for himself—that she had not been the one who'd been driving the car. Cynically he waited for her to say as much, and to implicate her friend whilst pleading her own innocence. It was obvious to him from the one assessing look with which he had taken in the whole of the scene in front of him that there was no way that this woman could have been the one driving his car; to anyone with even half a trained eye it was blindingly obvious that the other younger, over-made-up girl with her skimpy clothes and frightened, sullen face had been the driver. As he waited for the woman facing him to denounce her companion Marco fiercely reminded himself of all the reasons why he had been opposed to his cousin's marriage to his English model girlfriend.

Cross-cultural marriages were always, by the very necessity of their nature, bound to be more of a risk than those between people who shared the same background and upbringing. For those marriages to work both parties had to be dedicated to their love and to one another, to believe in it, to be one hundred and fifty per cent committed to it and to be mature and strong enough to make it work. That was a very tall order indeed in today's modern climate.

He himself had never been sexually promiscuous. He was too fastidious, too proud, too controlled to ever allow his appetites to control him, and it added to his already short temper to realise just how intense his physical reaction was to the woman standing in front of him.

'Are you the one who stole my car?' he demanded curtly, suddenly impatient to get the whole thing over and done with and the woman and her companion turned over to the police.

But, to his disbelief, instead of immediately denying that she was to blame and incriminating her friend, he heard her saying in a soft, shaky voice, 'Yes... Yes, I'm afraid... that...that it was me.'

As she heard herself confessing to a crime she most certainly had not committed Alice felt her heart lurch joltingly against her ribs. She still felt sick and dizzy and her heart was thumping erratically in panic. Panic because of the trouble she was going to be in, she quickly insisted to herself, and not in any way because of the effect the man standing watching her with that masklike, uninterpretable, assessing look was having on her.

Heavens, but he was formidable... Formidable and sexy... The sexiest man she had ever seen. So sexy in fact that he was making her feel...

'Yes?'

She could hear the fury in his voice as he repeated her admission. 'Yes?' he repeated as though he wanted to make sure he had heard her correctly. 'Yes, it was you?'

It was almost as though he wanted her to deny the crime, Alice thought dizzily. But why? So that he could indulge in the pleasure of berating her, accusing her of being a liar as well as a thief? Well, she wasn't going to give him that pleasure!

Bravely pushing to one side her own shock and fear, she told him firmly, 'Yes. It was I. I stole your car.'

She could hear Louise making a soft, moaning, hiccupping sound and instinctively Alice looked anxiously towards her.

The younger girl's tears had washed tracks of make-up from her face, giving her a clown-like appearance of vulnerable youthfulness, and as she saw the panic and fear in Louise's eyes Alice found her heart aching with compassion for her.

It must have given her a dreadful shock when they had crashed. No wonder she was looking so afraid. Instinctively, Alice felt protective towards her, overcoming her own feelings of shock and hostility towards the man confronting her and the feelings he was engendering within her to tell him quietly, 'I apologise for…what has happened and, of course, I will make good the damage to your car, but my…my…friend is very shocked. We are due to catch a flight home to England this afternoon, and we still have to collect our luggage from our hotel, so if there is some way in which we can expedite matters… I can give you all my details. My name is Alice Walsingham and…' She stopped as she saw the frown darkening his face as he listened to her.

'Your name is what?' he challenged her softly.

'Alice…Alice Walsingham,' Alice repeated, her voice starting to tremble a little as a feeling of foreboding rushed over her like a cold incoming tide.

Marco could hardly believe his ears. So this was the woman he had waited in vain to interview, this small scrap of female humanity with her slender body, her provocative breasts, her pale blonde hair, her far-too-pretty face, and her certainly far-too-dangerously potent effect on his hormones!

That such a thing should happen to him and with this

woman of all women! A woman who excited such interest
in the street from his own sex that a member of it was
unable to refrain from extolling the pleasure the sight of
her body gave him. A woman who had been an accomplice
to the theft of his car...a woman apparently so careless of
human life that she could have been an accomplice to an
accident of even more hideous and fatal proportions than
the one he had already had to endure. A woman who had
lied and implicated herself in a theft to protect the true
thief, who Marco could now see when he looked at her
properly was much younger than he had first thought. A
teenager, in fact. Against the urgings of his own self-
protective instincts, he found himself remembering certain
incidents from his cousin Aldo's youth, certain irrespon-
sible actions from which he, as Aldo's elder and family
mentor, had been obliged to extricate the younger man.

After all, he reminded himself with reluctant fair-
mindedness, he had seen the look of discomfort on Alice's
face when she had heard the ice-cream seller's full-bodied
compliment; and she had too looked shocked to the point
of actual nausea after the accident. As for the effect she
had on him!

The one thing about Alice that had caught his attention
when he'd read through her application and the letters of
recommendation that had accompanied it was the emotional input she put into caring for her charges. It was that
degree of involvement that he wanted for Angelina! He
had expected her to be an emotional woman, and one with
a deeply protective instinct, but what he had not anticipated and what he most certainly did not want was her
totally unexpected aura of sensuality! She wore it as lightly
and easily as though she herself was totally unaware of it,
which made it even more of a danger than if she had wantonly flaunted it, Marco recognised.

Grimly he turned to Louise. 'And you,' he questioned
her. 'You are?'

'Louise is in my charge,' Alice answered for her, assuming a firmness and authority she was far from feeling. She had bumped her head on the impact of the crash and it was aching horridly still and making her feel very poorly, but she had Louise to protect and that had to come before her own discomfort.

'She is only young and, as you can see, very upset. Her parents are expecting her return on this afternoon's flight and…it is my duty…my responsibility to see that she is on that flight.'

'Your duty…and your responsibility,' Marco emphasised. 'Where were those undoubtedly admirable virtues, I wonder, when you stole my car, risking not only your own lives, but those of other people as well? Have you any idea what a car smash can do, what carnage, what…destruction it can cause?' Marco demanded harshly as the nightmare images of the crash scene he had been called upon to witness when Aldo had driven away from the *palazzo* in the temper that had killed both him and his wife resurfaced.

With no way of knowing what he was thinking, Alice could feel her face starting to burn.

'I… It…I couldn't help myself,' she started to fib desperately. 'I have always loved…' Helplessly she looked at the car for inspiration, unable to remember in her panic just what kind of car it actually was…

Against his will Marco found himself being both intrigued and impossibly almost even amused as he witnessed her confusion as she hunted wildly for a rational explanation to cover both her behaviour and her protective fib. Anyone with any remote pretence to being a car lover would not have had to look wildly at the bonnet to realise what make of car they'd been driving.

'Maseratis,' he supplied dryly for her, his voice drowning out Louise's frantically whispered, 'Ferrari!'

'Yes. Maseratis,' Alice agreed, gratefully seizing on the name he had given her. 'Well, I've always loved them and when I saw yours, just couldn't resist. It was so tempting.

And you had left the keys in the ignition,' she told him reprovingly.

'So in effect it was my fault that you stole the car,' Marco suggested dryly.

She had the most revealing eyes, he decided, their colour a clear blue-green that was almost turquoise.

'Have you any idea just what his car means to an Italian man?' he asked her, speaking swiftly in Italian.

Without the slightest pause, she responded in the same language, telling him simply, 'I shouldn't have done it, I know.'

So she hadn't lied about her ability to speak his language, Marco recognised, and despite all reasons he knew he should summon the police and set about finding himself another nanny for Angelina, he knew that he was going to do no such thing.

A woman who for whatever reason was prepared to implicate herself in a crime to protect a younger person in her charge must have a protective instinct that would keep any child entrusted to her care safe and loved. And, so far as Marco was concerned, what Angelina needed more than anything else was just that very kind of security, even if it came wrapped up in a tantalising package with 'danger' written all over it!

'By rights I should summon the police and hand you both over to them,' he told Alice sternly, waiting for a few seconds as the colour drained from her face and she made a small, instinctive sound of protest and distress.

'However…you say that you are both booked on an afternoon flight back to England…but you,' he told her smoothly, 'or so I thought, were supposed to be being interviewed for a post here in Italy…'

Alice gaped at him. 'How do you know that?' she began, and then stopped as the unwanted, impossible, appalling truth began to seep hideously into her shocked brain.

'No!' she whispered, her eyes huge with despair.

'No. You can't be!'

'I can't be who?' Marco challenged her grimly.

Nervously Alice flicked her tongue-tip over her suddenly nervously dry lips, a gesture which Marco's eyes monitored whilst his body registered her action in a way that made him glad of the strength of will-power! Glad that it was strong enough to prevent him from covering the softness of her full lips with his own mouth. Richly pink, free of make-up, they reminded him unwantedly of the taut thrust of her nipples against her top.

Angrily he pushed his wanton thoughts away. He had neither the time to waste on self-indulgent analysis of them, nor the inclination to do so. Some things were best left undisturbed, unexamined… Her skin would be delicately pale, her breasts crowned with rose-red nipples and when he touched them with his lips she would…

As Alice heard him curse beneath his breath she jumped nervously. The heat beating down on her uncovered head was beginning to affect her. She felt confused and muzzy, and she wanted badly to be able to lie down somewhere cool—somewhere cool that did not include this formidable, sexy, downright disturbing man, she corrected herself shakily.

'I… My interview was with… I was supposed to be seeing…' she began to protest.

'Me,' Marco supplied for her with a softness that belied the steel-hard look he was giving her. 'Only you did not keep our appointment, which makes you unreliable as well as untrustworthy—and yet according to your agency…'

'I-I'm sorry I was late,' Alice began to stammer with what she knew to be ludicrous consternation. He thought she had stolen his car, after all, and here she was apologising for being late.

'To be late is an offence against the laws of good manners, and thus punishable by one's own conscience,' he agreed urbanely. 'But theft is an offence against the laws of the land and as such it is punishable by a term in prison…'

The way he was looking at her, his eyes now almost the colour of obsidian and just as empty of any kind of humane emotion as a piece of unfeeling stone, made her blood quite literally run icily cold in her veins. Shock and then fear crept over her in a painful tide. Prison! She knew that her fear showed in her face, and only her pride stopped her from protesting out loud.

Out of the corner of her eye she could see Louise, silent now, her shock as obvious as Alice's own in her suddenly very youthful, drawn white face.

As she struggled to find something to say a mobile phone started to ring imperiously. Almost as though she were observing the whole scene at a distance, Alice saw the man she now realised must be her once-prospective employer, the aristocratically named Conte di Vincenti, reaching to his pocket and removing his phone, swiftly responding to the call.

With her excellent grasp of Italian, Alice easily translated what he was saying and a fresh surge of anxiety seized her body, not this time for herself, but on behalf of the baby, whose sudden inexplicable and frightening sickness was the cause of the telephone call.

Swiftly instructing that a doctor was to be called, Marco ended the call, his face drawn into lines of harsh anxiety.

The nursemaid Angelina's mother had hired to look after the baby was not in his opinion a suitable person to have charge of such a young child. Bored and slovenly, she had no proper training for such a job, and so far as he could see no real love for the baby, but she was, apart from himself, the only person who was truly familiar to her and for that reason, until he found a suitable replacement nanny, he had felt unable to terminate her employment and send her back to Rome where he knew she would feel much more at home than in the Tuscan countryside.

It had been left to his housekeeper to telephone him and

advise him of baby Angelina's sickness. The *palazzo* was over an hour's fast drive away, and Marco had no time now to waste on a mere car accident in which mercifully no one had been hurt.

On Alice's CV had been the fact that she had some nursing experience, having done voluntary work in a local hospital, both as teenager and later too, when her employment commitments had allowed. Had it not been for his own too stubborn wariness where Englishwomen were concerned, Marco knew that Alice's obvious dedication to others would have inclined him towards selecting her as Angelina's nanny even over more highly qualified applicants.

However, now a new complication had entered the equation. The one thing that Marco had not been prepared for when he had mentally reviewed and tabulated the pros and cons of hiring Alice was that he himself might find her desirable! His reaction to her had caught him off guard. He had believed that he was armoured against any woman who was made in the same mould as the free-living, free-loving girl students he had encountered in England. So what was he saying? he asked himself sardonically, whilst he worried about Angelina.

That he could not control his own libido? No way!

Quickly Marco came to a decision. He would normally have been averse to having his hand forced by events, but now he wasn't concerned about that. He did not *want* to examine his decision more analytically—because of his concern for Angelina, he told himself. After all, his physical reaction to Alice was something he could control; baby Angelina's sickness was not.

'What time did you say your flight left?' he demanded.

White-faced with contempt and disbelief, Alice stared at him. What kind of man…what kind of father was he to give something as minor as a small car accident precedence over the health of his baby daughter? In his shoes the last thing she would have done would be to stand here, worrying about a mere car! Instead she would have been making her way as fast as she could to her baby's side.

So much for the myth that Italian men were wonderful fathers, who adored and protected their children!

Instinctively she felt a surge of desire to protect the baby and to castigate her father for his lack of concern; to show him just how contemptuous she felt of him in every way; as a trained professional, as an innocent victim of a crime she had not committed, and most of all as a woman.

A woman who had foolishly allowed herself to react to him in a way she was determined not to repeat!

Ignoring her throbbing headache, she accused him wildly, 'That poor baby! How can you be more concerned about your wretched car than her health?' Emotional tears filled her eyes, which she proudly refused to hide. She was not ashamed to show that she had normal human feelings, no matter how contemptuously that fact made him regard her. 'I thought that Italian men were supposed to love children,' she threw at him scornfully, unable to stop herself. 'But in your case it seems that your love of your car means more to you than the health of the baby.'

Something flickered in his eyes, an expression Alice could not quite catch, almost as though in some way her outburst had pleased him, but then as she focused more closely on him his expression changed, his hooded gaze seeming to deliberately conceal his reaction.

Turning his back on her, he flicked on his mobile and started issuing instructions into it.

When he had finished he turned back to her, and told her coolly, 'You are coming with me to the *palazzo*. Your…friend will be escorted to the airport and put on her flight home…'

Alice stared at him, hardly able to credit that she had heard him correctly. He was making her stay here, in Italy, at his home. Why? Shock, panic, fear, and a sharp, breath-snatching feeling she didn't want to name, but that she was forced to acknowledge came pretty close to a form of dangerous excitement, swirled the blood to her head. Was the heat of the Italian sun somehow affecting her brain?

It must be surely; there was no other acceptable explanation for that sharp, shocking, piercingly wanton feeling burning hotly through her body.

This man possessed none of the virtues she could ever want in a man; none of them, she insisted firmly to herself.

'You can't make me stay in Italy.' she began warningly.

She had already made up her mind that she was glad that she had not had the opportunity to be interviewed by him because there was totally no way she could ever countenance working for him.

His arrogance both infuriated and antagonised her, arousing emotions within her that she was totally unfamiliar with, making her feel, giddy, dizzy, dangerously close to losing her head. It was making her feel very much like a child exposed to danger, immediately wanting to run from it back to safety. She didn't like him. Not one little bit, but what she had just learned about his attitude towards his baby had aroused within her not just a furious sense of disgust and distaste for him as a man, but also an intense surge of pity for the small baby who was so dependent on him.

All she had been told about her prospective employment had been that she would have virtually sole charge of a six-month-old baby girl whose mother had recently died, and who needed a constant and loving female presence in her life.

That alone had been enough to make her yearn to provide her potential charge with all the protection and love she could give her. Those feelings were still there, intensified if anything by the cold-hearted manner of the little Angelina's father.

'You can't force us to do anything,' she responded forcefully.

'No?' Marco overrode her grimly. 'You have two choices, Alice Walsingham. Either you come with me now, or both you and your friend face the legal consequences of your crime. And to be honest I should have thought, having read your CV and the reports from your agency, that the decision would have been an easy and an automatic one for you. What was it they said about you? That you possessed an extremely strong nurturing instinct and a genuine love and concern for children? It seems to me that somewhere along the line you must have deceived them.'

Before she could speak in her own defence, Alice heard Louise give a faint sob of terror.

'Please, Alice,' the younger girl was beseeching her. 'Please, please do what he wants. I can't bear the thought of going to prison.'

As she listened to her Alice knew that in reality there was no choice for her at all. Not really.

There was no point in her making the mistake of hoping that the man in front of her was simply bluffing. She could see that he wasn't...

A large four-wheel-drive vehicle suddenly pulled up behind the red sports car. Its driver jumped out and came hurrying towards them.

Listening to the swift exchange of Italian between him and her persecutor, Alice realised that the new arrival worked for the *conte* and that the *conte* was instructing him to take care of the sports car, and escort Louise to the airport, whilst he, the *conte*, drove himself and Alice to his estate.

'Your luggage will be brought to the *palazzo* from the hotel,' he informed Alice, without bothering to ask her what her decision was. But then of course why should he? It must be as obvious to him as it was to her from Louise's white shocked face that there was no way she could subject the younger girl to the ordeal of police questioning and potentially a spell in prison, even if for her pride's sake she was prepared to inflict such traumas on herself.

There was barely time to do anything more than

exchange a swift hug with Louise, who was now sobbing woefully, full of contrition and guilt as she hugged Alice back with genuine appreciation and whispered, 'I'm so sorry. I never meant—'

'Shush, it's all right,' Alice whispered back to her, trying to reassure her, but still warning her gently, 'I don't think it would be a good idea to say anything about this to Connie.'

The last thing she wanted was for her sister to worry about her, especially since Connie had hinted to her that she and Steven were planning to try for a baby.

There was just time for them to exchange a final hug and then Alice was being firmly drawn away by her new employer. To an outsider she suspected that the hand he had placed around her upper arm looked as though he were merely guiding her. But she knew better. She could feel the sharp bite of those steely fingers against her flesh, she could tell too, from the closeness with which he held her to his side, that he was not in any way guiding her, but guarding her...as in imprisoning... She was his prisoner. He had total control over her, and she knew that he would not hesitate to exercise that control should he feel the need to do so.

Her whole body ached with shock. She felt slightly sick from the hot beat of the strong Florentine sunshine on her exposed head, and from what had happened. But there was no way she was going to show any sign of weakness in front of this man!

Had it not been for Louise and the plight of the baby she would certainly never have allowed him to dominate her like this. He was everything she hated in a man. Everything she despised and loathed.

Too arrogant, too sure of himself, too wrapped up in his own self-importance and too damn sexy by far. Oh, yes he was certainly that all right, she acknowledged, unable to resist the impulse to give him a quick sidelong look.

And then wishing she had not given in to such temptation as he caught her betraying glance, faultlessly returning it with a smooth, knowing response that made her face flame and her heart thud in denial of what she was feeling.

But even by turning away from him she wasn't able to escape; all she found was their reflections in the shop window. It seemed there was no way she could escape from him—nor from the shockingly intimate feelings he was making her experience.

Fiercely she tried to concentrate on realities, rather than feelings. He was much taller than her, imposingly so, his whole bearing proud and autocratic, his expression hardening the chiselled perfection of his features.

She in contrast looked small and pale, overwhelmed by him. He could have been a rapacious Roman centurion and she his captive. A long, dangerous shiver of an emotion she wasn't prepared to name shocked through her.

CHAPTER THREE

ALICE woke immediately at the first soft whimper of baby Angelina's cry despite the fact that it was almost three o'clock in the morning and she had had barely two hours' sleep.

They had arrived at the *palazzo* the previous afternoon, just as the full lazy heat of the June sunshine had been bathing the creamy walls of the huge Palladian building in hot golden light. Set as it was against a magnificent backdrop of the surrounding Tuscan countryside, the effect on Alice's finely tuned senses had almost overpowered her, affecting her as headily as too much indulgence in strong wine.

It was almost too perfect, had been her verdict as they had driven up the Lombardy-pine-guarded private road that led to the *palazzo*, and then in through the delicate high wrought-iron gates past imposingly formal gardens and finally into an enclosed courtyard at the rear of the *palazzo* which had immediately seemed to enclose her, shutting her off from the outside world and reality.

A small, gnarled man of about sixty had hurried out to the car, engaging in a low-voiced conversation with the *conte*, of which Alice could only hear the sharp, autocratic questions that her new employer was throwing at him.

'Yes, the doctor has been called,' Alice heard the older man replying in Italian. 'but there has been an emergency at the hospital and so he has not as yet arrived.'

'You have left the car in Florence?' Alice heard the older man asking the *conte*, in an incredulous tone that immediately raised Alice's hackles.

How typical of what she already knew of the *conte* that

36

even his employees should know that he would be more concerned about the future of his car than that of his baby!

'There was an accident,' she heard him replying grimly, shaking his head immediately as the other man instantly expressed concern for his health.

'No. It is all right, Pietro, I am fine,' the *conte* was assuring him.

Grittily, Alice watched him. At no point during their hair-raising drive to the *palazzo* had the *conte* expressed either interest or concern in whether or not she had been hurt in the accident, and she was certainly not going to tell him just how queasy and uncomfortable she had felt during the drive, she decided proudly.

She still felt rather weak, though, and she was relieved to be ushered into the cool interior of the *palazzo*, which was, as she had somehow known it would be, decorated in an elegant and very formal style, and furnished with what she suspected were priceless antiques.

How on earth could a young child ever feel at home in a place like this? she wondered ruefully, as she followed the *conte* and his housekeeper, Pietro's wife, Maddalena, who had now joined them, through several reception rooms and into a huge formal entrance hall from which a flight of gleaming marble stairs rose imposingly upward.

The baby's suite of rooms—there was in Alice's opinion no other way to describe the quarters that had been set aside for the little girl; certainly they were far too grand to qualify for the word 'nursery' as she understood it— was at one end of a long corridor, and furnished equally imposingly as the salons she had already seen.

A nervous and very flustered young girl who was quite plainly terrified of the *conte* appeared from one of the other rooms in response to the *conte*'s voice. She was inexpertly clutching the baby, who was quite plainly in discomfort and crying.

Immediately Alice's training and instincts took over, and without waiting for anyone's permission she stepped forward and firmly removed the baby from the girl's anxious grip.

The baby smelled of vomit and quite plainly needed a nappy change. Her face was red and blotchy from distress and as Alice gently brushed her cool fingers against her skin, whilst reassuringly comforting her, she suspected that she probably had a temperature.

Out of the corner of her eye she saw the move the *conte* made towards her as she took control and cradled the baby against her shoulder. Automatically she turned towards him, only just managing to suppress a small smile of grim contempt as she saw him glance from the baby to his own immaculate clothes.

A truly loving father seeing his motherless child in such distress should have instinctively placed the baby's need for the security of his arms above those of his immaculate suit, especially when she suspected that the *conte* was more than wealthy enough to buy a whole wardrobe of designer suits.

A baby, though, could never be replaced; nor, in Alice's opinion, could a baby ever be given too much love or security. And she immediately made a silent but vehement vow that, just so long as it was within her power to do so, she would ensure that little Angelina never, ever lacked for love.

As she and the baby made eye contact Alice felt a soft, small tug of emotion pulling on her heartstrings, her feelings reflecting openly in her eyes and quite plain for the man watching her to see and comprehend.

He had heard of love at first sight, Marco acknowledged wryly, and now had witnessed it taking place.

Quickly he veiled his own gaze to prevent Alice from seeing what he was thinking.

Almost as soon as she held her, little Angelina stopped crying as though she had instinctively recognised the sure, knowing touch of someone who knew what she was doing.

Alice could hear the *conte* speaking to the nursemaid in

Italian. Alice wondered why a man as wealthy as the *conte* might choose to employ an untrained nanny to look after his motherless child. The girl looked haggard and white-faced and she had started to wring her hands as she explained how the baby had started to be violently sick, shortly after she had fed her.

Alice had already made her own professional diagnosis of what she suspected was wrong. Quietly but determinedly she walked towards the communicating door through which the nursemaid had appeared.

The room beyond it, whilst as elegantly furnished as the one she had been in, was in total chaos, and Alice grimaced as she saw the pile of soiled baby things heaped up on the floor, and the general untidiness of the room. It was plain to her that the girl whom the *conte* had left in charge of his baby daughter had no professional skills and very probably very little experience with babies.

Carrying Angelina into the bathroom adjoining the bedroom, she quickly started to prepare a bath for her, all the time holding her securely in one arm, sensing her fear and need to be held.

It astonished her when the *conte* suddenly appeared at her side, instructing her, 'Give her to me.'

The baby started to cry again, a small, thin, grizzling cry of exhaustion, pain and misery. Dubiously Alice looked at her unwanted employer, but before she could say anything the baby turned her head and looked at the *conte* and suddenly she stopped crying, her eyes widening in recognition and delight as she held out her arms towards the man watching her.

To her own furious outrage, Alice actually felt sharp, emotional tears start to prick her eyes at this evidence of the baby's love for her father. But what really shocked her was the easy way in which the *conte* had held his small daughter; whilst she prepared a bath for her, cradling her lovingly in his arms, soothing her with soft murmurs of reassurance until Alice was ready to take Angelina off him and gently remove her soiled clothes.

'I think that she may only be suffering from a bad bout of colic,' she told the *conte* as she gently lowered the baby into the water, keeping her attention on her all the time to ensure that she was not becoming in any way distressed, 'but of course I would advise that she is checked over by a doctor.'

What she did not want to say was that she thought that it could be the inexpert handling of the baby by her nurse that was responsible for her agitated state. How could any-one leave such a young child with someone who was quite plainly not qualified to look after her?

Surely, having lost his wife, the *conte* would want to do everything he could to protect and nurture her child? A child who, it was already obvious to Alice, was looking helplessly to her father for love and security.

The arrival of the doctor interrupted her private thoughts, and whilst he was looking at the baby the *conte* had dismissed the nursemaid to go downstairs and have her supper, an act of apparent kindness, which for some reason only added to Alice's resentment of him. He had shown no concern at all for the fact that she had not eaten in hours. Not that she wanted to eat particularly; she still felt slightly nauseous and suspected that she might still be suffering from shock. But just whether that shock had been caused by the accident or by the *conte* himself, Alice was not prepared to consider.

The doctor quickly confirmed Alice's own diagnosis that the baby was suffering from colic and was probably also slightly dehydrated. Surprisingly he openly admon-ished the *conte* for allowing such an obviously inexperi-enced girl to have charge of Angelina.

'I understand what you are saying, Doctor,' the *conte* had accepted, 'but I have had no real choice in the matter. The girl was chosen to take charge of Angelina by her mother. She has been with her since the first weeks of her birth, and I have been reluctant to remove her from the care of someone so familiar, although I have now taken steps to rectify the situation since, like you, I have been concerned about the girl's ability to be responsible for the needs of such a small child.

'Miss Walsingham here has been employed by me to take over full charge of the nursery and of Angelina,' he told the doctor, turning to indicate Alice. 'She is English, as Angelina's mother was, and a fully qualified nanny.'

The doctor looked at Alice appraisingly, before turning to say with very Italian male appreciation, to Alice, 'May I say how fortunate I consider Angelina to be to have such a pretty companion.' The avuncular smile he gave her before turning back to the *conte*, along with the twinkle in his eye, reassured Alice that he was simply being gallant.

'You will have trouble on your hands, I'm afraid, my friend,' he continued to the *conte*.

'I do not know whether to commiserate with you or envy you for having so much distracting temptation beneath your roof.'

Alice felt her face starting to burn. What on earth was the doctor trying to imply...? That the *conte* might be tempted. By her?

However, before she was able to formulate her own thoughts, the *conte* himself responded to the doctor, telling him with razor-sharp crispness, 'I have employed Miss Walsingham for her professional qualities as a nanny, and not because of her looks, and as for her ability to tempt our sex... Miss Walsingham's contract with me precludes her from encouraging any hot-blooded and foolish young man to be tempted by her.'

The hard-eyed look he gave her scorched Alice's skin.

'And since she has already foolishly exhibited to me just how irresistible she finds temptation, I fully intend to ensure that her will-power gets all the support it might need, and in whatever form she might need it.'

Alice gasped. How dared he take such a high-handed

attitude with her, and in front of someone else? She was acutely aware of the interested way in which the doctor was now studying both of them, his dark eyes twinkling as though he found something amusing in the situation. Well, he might do so, but Alice most certainly did not.

However, before she was able to speak the *conte* continued almost brusquely, 'It is essential that Angelina has stability in her life. She has already lost far too much…' His voice had become so sober that immediately Alice felt unable to take issue with him regarding the statement he had just made.

'Ah, yes, that was a terrible tragedy indeed,' the doctor agreed gravely as he finished his examination of the baby and handed her back to Alice.

To her astonishment, as she reached out to take the baby the *conte* forestalled her, taking hold of his daughter himself and saying over Alice's head to the doctor, 'Miss Walsingham was involved in a thankfully minor accident earlier today, and I think it would be a good idea if you were to check her over…'

'No. There's no need. I'm fine,' Alice responded immediately, bridling at the *conte*'s inference that she was almost as incapable of making her own decisions as the baby he was cradling against his shoulder with fatherly expertise.

At some point he had removed his jacket, and the fine white cotton of his shirt did very little to conceal the dark muscularity of the torso that lay beneath it. Alice could even see the shadowing of his body hair. And she actually felt her muscles threaten to go weak. Fortunately she was able to tense them against such betrayal as she forced herself to focus on the waiting doctor and not her employer.

'I am perfectly all right,' she insisted.

And it was, after all, the truth. That nauseous headache she was still suffering had simply been caused by the heat and her own intense emotions. The minute bruise she had sustained was luckily concealed by her hair, and there really hadn't been any need for the *conte* to draw attention to her health!

Quite why she felt so resentful and hostile towards his apparent concern for her health, she didn't know. Perhaps it had something to do with the anger she felt towards him that he could actually employ a woman he considered to be guilty of attempted theft to look after his daughter— who surely should matter far, far more to him than any mere material possession!

Reflecting now in the middle of the night on what had been said then, Alice reminded herself that the agency had told her before she'd left London that her prospective employer was looking for her to make a long-term commitment to her charge, and that she would be asked to sign a contract to that effect, but she had overlooked that fact in the turmoil of the accident and its aftermath. Now, however…

Quickly she got out of her bed and walked across to Angelina's cot. She was the reason that Alice was now awake, her instincts alert to the baby's distress even in her sleep. Angelina was lying awake, whimpering softly. Gently Alice lifted her out, checking her temperature and her nappy.

Her skin felt reassuringly cool, but her nappy needed changing, and Alice decided this would be a good opportunity to give her a small extra feed.

She suspected that she was slightly underweight and maybe even a little malnourished. If she was a slow feeder, then her young nurse might have become impatient.

Holding her tenderly against her shoulder, she padded into the room adjacent to the nursery proper, which had been converted into a temporary but very well-equipped kitchen, with everything to meet the baby's needs.

She had already prepared some bottles of formula before going to bed, and as she removed one from the fridge and started to heat it she studied the baby's face.

Her mother might have been English but she looked completely Italian. She had her father's dark hair and eyes, and Alice suspected she had also inherited the *conte*'s determined chin.

For a baby of six months she was a little on the small side. As she looked at her with grave, worried eyes Alice couldn't resist dropping a tender kiss on her forehead as she smoothed her baby curls.

She was adorable, but so vulnerable. Alice ached to protect and care for her; so much so, in fact, that she could almost actually feel a soft tug on her own womb as she held her.

Poor baby. No mother and a father who couldn't possibly love her as she needed to be loved.

In his own bedroom, Marco frowned as he heard over the intercom the soft, cooing sounds of love and tenderness that Alice was making to the baby.

He, like her, had woken at the first sound of Angelina's distress. His concern over the nursemaid's ability to take proper care of the baby had led to him having a sophisticated baby-alarm system installed in the nursery suite so that he could hear if Angelina cried.

Indeed he had been halfway towards the bedroom door when he had realised that Alice had picked her up.

He'd employed Alice primarily so that Angelina would have someone else to bond with other than himself, but also to give himself the freedom to concentrate on his busy professional life, so now he was surprised to recognise that he actually felt almost a little put out at the speed with which the baby was responding to her.

Alice Walsingham!

What was it about this pale, infuriating Englishwoman that was making him feel such ridiculous and unwanted things? Showing him such intimate and dangerous images; images of her lying beneath him in the soft heat of a summer night, her blonde hair spread against his pillows as he threaded his fingers through it and held her so that he could kiss that tempting mouth of hers into reciprocal passion; images of her holding a dark-haired child in her arms, a boy child who was not Angelina, but his child!

Marco didn't know whether to laugh or cry at his own folly.

Alice was a young woman who was quite obviously not very good at hiding her feelings, and he had seen the wariness and hostility in her eyes when she looked at him!

Those were feelings he would be wise to allow her to indulge in—for both their sakes.

There was a considerable amount of discreet family pressure on him to marry. He was after all the head of the family, but as yet…

Marriage. Now why on earth had thinking about Alice Walsingham sent his thoughts in that direction?

He belonged to the modern century and there was no way he could ever feel comfortable in any kind of 'arranged' marriage, but, on the other hand, at thirty-five he had seen enough marriages and relationships go wrong to feel a certain cynical wariness about the permanence of what his contemporaries called 'love'.

Against his will he suddenly found himself thinking that his mother would have liked Alice.

He could hear the soft sucking noises Angelina was making as Alice fed her, and with shocking, nerve-wrenching immediacy he was suddenly once again visualising her holding a baby in her arms, her face soft with maternal love, her breasts bare…

Grimly he banished the image. That was not the way he wanted to see her, not even in the privacy of his own thoughts, and it was most certainly not the way he wanted or intended to think of her.

He was a man, he reminded himself, and it was a long time since he had had a sexual relationship with a woman. Maybe so, but that had not bothered him until now.

In fact, when presented with the opportunity to rectify

such an omission, as he had been on many, many occasions, he had not felt the slightest inclination to take it, so why was he now thinking about a woman whom he had only met a matter of hours ago in such an intimate and specific way?

Grimly Marco looked at his watch.

It was four o'clock in the morning. He had to be in Florence at ten for an important meeting; right now what he should be doing was sleeping and not giving in to the folly of turning his newest employee into some kind of fantasy madonna.

Alice waited until the baby was a heavy sleeping weight in her arms before returning her to her cot. Gently laying her in it, she watched her for several minutes.

Just looking at her made her heart ache so. She knew it was totally unprofessional of her to get so involved, but she just couldn't help herself. All babies needed and deserved to be loved, but this one especially so, she decided fiercely. After all, she had the double burden of having lost her mother and having as her father the most coldly autocratic and unemotional, dislikeable man Alice had ever met!

The baby was asleep and so should she be. She still felt muzzy and headachy but it was too much effort to bother taking anything. After checking on Angelina one more time, she made her way back to her own bed.

CHAPTER FOUR

ALICE watched in loving concern as Angelina opened her eyes and looked at her with bewilderment and confusion as she realised that she was a stranger to her.

It was seven o'clock in the morning and Maria the nursemaid was hovering behind her. Quietly Alice moved away from the cot so that Angelina could see her familiar face, but, instead of looking relieved when she saw her, the baby started to cry.

Immediately Alice picked her up, soothing her, feeling the panicky thud of her tiny heart start to ease as she accepted the loving reassurance of Alice's arms around her.

Sulkily Maria declared, 'The baby, she does not like me.' Tossing her head, she announced, 'She is not a good baby. I stay with her only because I need the money. And because of her poor mother.' She crossed herself as she spoke, watching as Alice heated Angelina's morning bottle of formula. 'She will not drink her milk. She is very difficult,' she warned Alice. 'I shall be glad to go back to Roma.'

'Rome!' Alice exclaimed.

'That is where I was working, as a…a housemaid when her mother told me that she needed someone to help her with her baby. She said that she could not look after her on her own and her father, he was no good. He did not care about the baby. They argued about it all the time. She wished that she had not married him. She told me so. He was very unkind to her.

'There were many arguments. She did not want to have the baby. She showed me many photographs of when she was in England, wearing pretty clothes.'

The picture her gossip was drawing for Alice was not a happy one, and Alice knew that she should stop her from speaking so openly about the marital problems of the *conte* and his late wife, but against her will she found that she was listening to her, her indignation darkening her eyes as she reflected on the selfishness of her charge's parents.

'It is tragic that Angelina's mother was killed,' was all she would allow herself to say.

'Tragic, yes,' the nursemaid agreed, giving a dismissive shrug as she told her, 'Before the accident they had quarrelled very badly. She had drunk much wine. She told me that she was going to leave him once they got back to Roma.'

Alice tried not to show how appalled she was by the maid's revelations. How could the *conte* have behaved in such a way to his wife, the mother of his child? A child that neither of them had wanted, according to the nursemaid, who seemed to know in very intimate detail about the lives of her employers.

'Poor baby,' Alice couldn't help murmuring as she started to feed Angelina. 'To have lost her mother and to have such an uncaring father.'

'Yes, he was uncaring, that one,' the nursemaid agreed.

As Alice had suspected, Angelina was a slow feeder, but Alice did not try to rush her, coaxing and praising her and feeling herself melt with pleasure when she finally rewarded her with an empty bottle and an unexpected smile.

She had sent Maria downstairs with the baby's dirty laundry—later in the day she would speak to the housekeeper about it herself, but right now she was enjoying having Angelina to herself. She was just in the middle of telling her joyfully what a clever, clever baby she was when the nursery door opened and the *conte* walked in.

The moment she saw him Alice could feel all her antagonism and hostility towards him surging through her. This was a man who had quarrelled so badly with his wife that she had driven to her death; a man who had apparently neither loved nor wanted his child.

She tensed as he came towards her, standing so close to her that she could feel the cool, silky brush of his shirt sleeve against her bare arm.

'How is she this morning?' he asked Alice as he frowned down at the baby in her arms.

'She is tired, but she has finished her feed,' she responded automatically.

'She slept through the night?'

The unexpectedness of the question caught her off guard.

'Well, no…she didn't…but then I didn't expect her to do so,' she told him almost defensively. 'I am a stranger to her. And she has not been well. She must be so confused, poor baby. She has had so many changes in her life already.'

'Which is why I stressed to your agency that I want you to make a long-term commitment to Angelina. That commitment, as I am sure they will have informed you, requires you to sign a contract that would bind you to being Angelina's nanny for the next five years. I have to say that I find it…unusual that a woman like you should be prepared to make such a commitment.' He paused and looked at her so slowly and deliberately that Alice knew that both her colour and her temper were rising. What did he mean 'a woman like you'? She itched to challenge him, but her training refused to allow her to do so. However, no amount of training could prevent her from giving an angry little hiss when he continued smoothly, 'After all, even if there is no man in your life right now…' He stopped and looked at her in a way that made Alice fume with indignation. 'Unfortunately,' he told her grimly, 'the Italian male has a weakness for women of your colouring, even though experience has shown me that relationships between people of different cultures are beset by difficult problems. And it does not help the situation that so many Northern

European women seem to view Italian men as hot-blooded, romantic lovers, who are ruled more by their emotions than by their brains.'

Alice couldn't control her outrage any longer. She was a professional woman, here in her professional capacity, not some silly girl looking for romance. And if that was what he thought of her, why had he ever chosen to consider her for the job in the first place? But before she could voice her indignation the *conte* was continuing coolly, 'I must admit I had assumed from the photograph your agency sent me that you were far less...sensual-looking than has proved to be the case.'

Sensual-looking? Her? Alice didn't know whether to be offended or bemused.

It was true that the photographs the agency had of her were two years out of date, and portrayed her with her hair neatly drawn back off her face, and that the first time the *conte* had seen her she had been wearing it loose. It was probably also true that the fortnight she had spent in Dubai in the spring with her previous employers had turned her beige-blonde hair several shades lighter, and that life and the effect of running after two energetic young boys had honed her body down a dress size, but that was hardly her fault; and nor, surely, was it likely to make her attractive to the average male who would surely prefer his women on the voluptuously curvaceous side?

'Five years is a long time for a woman of your age to—' the *conte* continued, but Alice refused to let him finish his sentence.

'To what?' she challenged him sharply. The conversation they were engaged in was a dangerous one. Her instincts told her that and they were telling her something else as well. Something she really did not want to acknowledge or hear. Something that was making her pulse race and beginning to fuel an unfamiliar and heady sense of excitement—like the frothiness of champagne laced with the dark allure of a highly intoxicating spirit—and she, as she warned herself sternly, had no head for such things.

Her body, though, didn't seem prepared to listen to the wise cautioning of her brain! The stark, brooding look he was giving her made her toes curl and her heart lurch dangerously against her ribs.

What was he trying to imply?

'You are not a nun who has taken vows of celibacy,' he told her pointedly, 'and it is only natural that you should want—'

Alice had heard enough!

'What I want,' she told him explicitly, 'is to be allowed to do the job I have been employed for, which, as I understand it, is to bring some measure of stability, love and security in the life of a six-month-old baby who has suffered the unimaginable trauma of losing her mother. And if you think for one moment that I have come to Italy for any other purpose—' She gave him a scornful, proud look, driven into the kind of frankness she would normally have felt far too inhibited and self-controlled to express.

'I am a modern woman, *Conte*, and I can assure you that the last thing on my mind is either idle flirtation, or trying to find myself a husband.'

'It said on your CV that you love children.'

His comment caught her off guard.

'Yes, I do,' she agreed, frowning. Maybe, for some reason he had changed his mind about employing her, perhaps because of what had happened the previous day. If his conscience was pricking him about the irresponsibility of entrusting his daughter to a woman who, so far as he knew, had stolen his car, then that was one thing, but if he thought she was going to allow him to question her dedication to her work, then…

The length of his silence and the way he was looking at her made tiny trickles of nerve-pricking sensation quiver through her body.

'Well, surely, that being the case, it is only natural that
at some stage you should want to give birth to your own.'

Alice opened her mouth and then closed it again. Of
course she hoped some day to have her own family, and
to have it with a man she loved and who loved her, but
that lay in the future!

It occurred to her that what he was saying to her might
simply be an unorthodox way of testing her dedication to
her job. If so, he was about to find out just how dedicated
and committed she was! There was only one baby in her
life at the moment and that baby was his!

Somewhere deep inside Alice a small, urgent voice tried
to make itself heard, but Alice was too angrily indignant
to heed it. Her professional pride was at stake now!

'I am perfectly prepared to sign the contract, and to
commit myself to Angelina, legally, for the next five
years,' she told him swiftly.

Prepared to sign it; she wanted to sign it; after all she
was already committed emotionally to Angelina, and nothing—nothing—would tempt her into abandoning the baby
into the sole care of her patently uncaring father!

Against his will Marco found that he was focusing on
the indignant heaving of her breasts as she glared furiously
at him. They made him ache to cup them in his hands and
see if they felt as soft and sweetly rounded as they looked.

Determinedly he averted his gaze, but not before Alice's
body had recognised his interest, and, as though somehow
that knowledge had sent a secret message to her senses, to
her chagrin she suddenly felt her nipples harden and peak,
provocatively thrusting against the delicate fabric of her
top, just as they had done on the first occasion on which
she had seen him.

She could feel her face burning with shame and anger.
How could this be happening to her? She simply wasn't
the sort of person who…to…be like this!

To her relief Marco was turning away from her, demanding, 'Very well, then, we shall go straight down to my study where you can read and then sign the contract...'

However, as Alice made to follow him to the door he stopped her, asking coldly, 'Haven't you forgotten something?'

And then to her chagrin he strode back towards the cot where the sleeping baby lay, leaving Alice to hurry after him.

'Don't wake her,' she whispered as he leaned into the cot to look at the baby. 'She needs her sleep.'

'I wasn't going to wake her,' he whispered back reprovingly. 'I simply wished to check that she was all right.'

As he spoke his voice softened and to her amazement as she looked at him Alice realised that he was actually smiling at the sleeping baby. And then, even more amazingly given what she knew about him, he drew the gentlest of tender fingertips against the baby's soft cheek, before blowing her a kiss.

It was all done so unselfconsciously and so lovingly that Alice knew that if she hadn't known better and her only observation of his parenting skills had been that one she would have immediately assumed that he was a loving and caring father.

'Oh, by the way,' he instructed her as she followed him out of the nursery, 'the senior members of my household address me by my Christian name of Marco. I wish you to do the same.'

Marco. Alice could feel the shape of it filling her mouth, its sound, soft and yet hard at the same time, velvet cloaking steel, unlike the man himself who was quite unmistakably steel on steel with no softening covering at all!

It disturbed Alice to have to acknowledge the effect he was having on her.

Dislike, that was what it was, she assured herself hastily, but still a feeling she did not want to name coiled itself around her heart, as insidious and dangerous as a serpent waiting to strike a mortal bite.

'I have to go out this morning. If Angelina shows any signs of being poorly, please call the doctor immediately. My housekeeper, Maddalena, will give you his number.'

As she followed him along the corridor and then down the imposing flight of marble stairs Alice reminded herself that it was for Angelina's sake that she was staying here. The baby needed her, and there was no way that Alice could abandon her.

Not now!

Marco's study was reached through a series of breathtakingly beautifully furnished ante-rooms, but, to Alice's surprise, once he opened the door to it and ushered her inside she saw that the study itself was unexpectedly plainly furnished—plainly, but very stylishly and expensively, she guessed shrewdly as she caught sight of the Pollock paintings on one wall, and observed the clean lines of the room's furniture.

It was a man's room, and the room of a particular man, she recognised, a room which initially looked as though it were a designer's set piece but which on closer inspection proved to have many small personal details: a cast footprint, which she guessed must be Angelina's; the bust of a man whose features were somehow familiar, although she didn't realise why until she heard Marco saying, 'My father. He and my mother were killed in a plane accident. My uncle, his younger brother, was flying the machine at the time and he and my aunt were also killed.'

Alice could hear her own indrawn breath of shock.

What he had just told her made him so much more human...so...so vulnerable. But she didn't want to think of him like that; didn't want to feel her heartstrings pulled on his behalf.

'It was my father who encouraged me to train as an architect,' he continued, more as though he was talking to himself than to her. 'He said that although one day I would inherit from him, I needed to make a life for myself, and not simply sit around waiting for his shoes, especially since it would be a long wait.'

Alice could hear the pain in his voice.

'I wish that might have been so.'

He could talk about the loss of his parents, and show her the pain he obviously still felt at their loss, Alice reflected, but he seemed totally impervious to the loss of his wife. Not even when he was talking about Angelina, her baby, did he mention her. Because that wound was too raw, or because he felt guilty about her death?

She watched as he opened a desk drawer and removed some papers.

'This is your contract,' he informed her, his eyebrows snapping together as he saw that she was still standing several feet away from his desk.

'It will be easier for me to point out the more important clauses in it if you come and stand here,' he instructed her, gesturing to the space beside him.

Reluctantly Alice moved towards him.

The air in the room had felt fresh and pleasantly cool when she had first walked into it, but now all at once she felt hot, unable to breathe properly, suffocatingly aware when she did do so that she was breathing in air that held a dangerously intimate male scent.

She tensed as Marco moved closer to her, putting the typed document down on the desk between them, waiting until she had read it before saying, 'If you are satisfied you understand and accept everything the contract contains, then please sign it.'

Silently Alice did so, watching as he added his signature to hers.

'So,' he told her softly. 'You are now in my employ and committed to Angelina's future.'

She started to move away from him, stopping as she caught her hip on the corner of the desk to let out a small sound of pain. Immediately he was turning towards her, asking what was wrong. She started to assure him that it was nothing, but to her consternation he reached out and touched her hip, his fingertips cool and impersonal against her skirt-clad body.

His touch might be impersonal but her reaction to it, to him, most certainly wasn't, she thought, realising her face was flaming.

She felt him tense, and then suddenly curse beneath his breath before reaching for her, imprisoning her upper arms within the firm grip of his lean fingers as he turned her in towards his own body.

Alice knew immediately what was going to happen. After all, hadn't she shamingly imagined it already a dozen, no, a hundred, times in the deepest and most private recesses of her secret thoughts? She could feel the frantic racing of her own heartbeat, and she could feel too the heavy malely aroused thud of his.

She reached out to try to stop him but when her hands encountered the fine smoothness of his cotton shirt, somehow of their own volition they spread out against it. Beneath her splayed fingertips she could feel the hardness of the torso his shirt concealed. Flesh, muscle, bone and hair, that was all it was—he was... Dizzily she closed her eyes.

All... It was everything. He was everything!

Was she going totally insane?

Frantically she opened them again and looked up, her gaze immediately enmeshed in the hot, golden-eagle-eyed shimmer of his.

Like a bird of prey he was transfixing her. 'No,' she whispered as she saw him lowering his head towards her own, but it was already too late and his mouth caught hers on the soft open plea, stealing her breath, silencing her objection.

His lips felt cool and firm against her own, their touch sending darkly chaotic thoughts and desires tumbling through her; their movement against her mouth was knowing and experienced, first subduing her desire to fight and then luring, tantalising, tormenting her into giving him the self-betraying response he wanted. Why was it that just that mere brush of his mouth on hers could make her want to move so much closer to him; make her want to cling to him; make her want to hold onto him and keep his mouth on hers for ever?

The hands that had been imprisoning her were no longer doing so, instead one of them was curled behind her neck, supporting it, whilst the fingers of the other were entwined in her hair, holding her still in willing enthralment to the mastery of his kiss.

Enthralment?

Her body was on fire…aching…longing…but somehow she found her panic gave her the strength to drag herself back from the brink of the precipice luring her.

Pulling herself free of Marco, she demanded with unguarded emotion, 'What…why did you do that?'

The look he was giving her made her shiver. It was deep, dark, hooded and unfathomable.

As he looked at her Marco wondered what she would do if he told her the truth, which was that he had kissed her because he had simply had no option.

Feigning a coolness he was far from feeling, he told her, 'I did it because you and I both know that it's what you've been waiting for me to do from the first moment I saw you. It was inevitable that it would happen, and, that being the case, it will make life simpler for both of us that we have got it out of the way.'

Alice could scarcely believe her ears.

'No,' she rejected immediately, 'that isn't true. I never…'

'Yes,' Marco overrode her. 'When I saw you in the street eating your ice cream, you looked at my mouth as though it was me you wanted to taste, and perhaps now that I've satisfied your curiosity we can…'

Alice felt close to tears. How dared he suggest that she...?

'No.' She refused to back down, to be bullied into accepting the blame for what he had begun. 'You were the one who looked at me...at...at my breasts,' she accused him wildly.

She would never normally have been so forthright, but he was forcing her to do so in order to protect herself...

'Because I wanted to taste them?' he suggested softly. He gave a small shrug. 'Very well, then, perhaps I did. Your top fitted very snugly and your breasts...' Deliberately he allowed his voice to trail away meaningfully.

Alice went white. This just wasn't the kind of conversation she was used to. Her body felt hot...cold...her mind and her emotions in total turmoil. How could he stand there so coolly, when she felt so...so...?

She couldn't work for him now, no way. Her glance fell to the contract she had just signed and, as though he had read her mind, he told her softly, 'I'm afraid it's too late for second thoughts now, and for regrets... You are committed.'

CHAPTER FIVE

COMMITTED! She was that all right, Alice acknowledged a couple of hours later as she turned away from what she was doing to smile at the baby who lay kicking happily on the baby mat that Alice had spread on the floor for Angelina to play on whilst she set about bringing order to the untidy nursery.

Already Angelina was gripping her new nanny's heart in her small baby fist, and Alice knew there was no way she was going to prise those small, dependent, but oh-so-strong little fingers free...and no way she really wanted to. But when it came to Angelina's father...

She shuddered as she remembered that scene in his study. How could she have behaved like that? She didn't know. She didn't want to know. Far better to simply put the whole thing right out of her mind. Far, far better.

But could she do that? She must, she told herself frantically. She had to. For Angelina's sake and her own.

Alice had spent the morning keeping a careful check on her new charge, gently encouraging her to get used to her as she cuddled and talked to her, in between checking over the nursery's equipment.

The drawers full of new and exquisite baby clothes made her catch her breath—in dismay rather than admiration; lovely though everything was, these were what Alice privately called 'dress-up clothes'. The type that in a traditional aristocratic family a baby would be dressed in to be passed around from one elderly relative to another—there was nothing remotely practical. Nothing a baby could wear to stretch or play or grow or experience life in. What had also struck her as slightly odd was the fact that the clothes virtually all appeared to be new; as though they had been purchased *en masse* and by someone who had no real hands-on experience of what a baby actually needed.

In fact it seemed to Alice that everything in the nursery was new. The expensive soft toys sitting neatly on top of one of the dressers looked beautiful, but they would do nothing to encourage a six-month-old to acquire and practise new skills. It seemed plain to Alice that whoever had chosen these clothes and toys did not really have an informed idea of what a baby needed. Beautiful hand-embroidered clothes and traditional long dresses were fine for high days and holidays, but where were the dungarees, the tee shirts, and the robust clothes that an active baby needed?

At lunchtime Marco's housekeeper, Maddalena, arrived to introduce herself and to inform Alice that she was having a light lunch sent up to the nursery for her since Marco had informed her that Alice would be dining with him later in the day.

Dining with him! Shakily Alice digested this nerve thrilling information before telling Maddalena, 'I haven't seen Maria since earlier this morning. Do you know where she is?'

'Probably in Roma by now,' the housekeeper replied grimly, adding, 'She came downstairs and telephoned her boyfriend there, and when she had finished she told me that she didn't want to stay here any longer.'

Alice was not really surprised that the girl had left. She had expressed to Alice her dislike of the quietness of the *palazzo*, and her preference for the city, and it had been obvious that she was not really attached to Angelina.

Maddalena continued, 'Not that she is any loss. Not really up to the job. But knowing the mother...' She stopped, her mouth pursing disapprovingly.

'The accident must have been a dreadful shock for all of you,' Alice said gently and tactfully.

The housekeeper shrugged.

'As to that, we hardly knew her. She didn't like the *palazzo*. She preferred Roma. And then when she did come here! Well, all I know is that she left here in a temper, screaming that she had never wanted the child and that she was ruining her life. What kind of mother is it that leaves her baby like that, I ask you?' the housekeeper demanded indignantly of Alice.

'Angelina has two parents,' Alice felt bound to point out. The housekeeper was certainly painting a very unflattering description of Marco's wife, but there were always two sides to every story, Alice reminded herself. Who could say without knowing her just what had driven her to behave so recklessly?

'Ppff… The father was as bad as the mother was.'

Alice could hardly believe her ears. The last thing she had expected was for the housekeeper to actually criticise Marco and to her, a new employee.

'It is just as well that you are here. The poor little one needs someone to take proper care of her. That maid…' The housekeeper gave a dismissive shake of her head. 'She is no loss to anyone, least of all little Angelina…'

The housekeeper had gone before Alice could question her about whether or not Angelina possessed any other clothes.

His meeting over, Marco opened his briefcase and removed a letter that had arrived before he had left for the city. He had already read it, but he felt the need to read it again.

It was from Pauline Levinsky, the woman who had been Alice's employer prior to her coming to work for him. Marco had approached her through Alice's agency, wanting to check out her opinion of Alice as a nanny.

Her letter began with an apology for not replying to him earlier, explaining that she had relocated to New York and that his letter had been redirected to her.

It went on to tell him that, whilst she had no wish to alarm him, she felt she ought to warn him that although Alice had cared for her two sons, diligently and carefully, she had discovered that Alice had been sleeping with her husband. She had written:

Of course, to some of these modern girls having sex has no more meaning than exchanging handshakes. It's just a game they play. Notches on the bedpost. How many men they can seduce. Since Alice had already tendered her notice, there seemed little point in threatening her with dismissal, although with hindsight I suppose I should have reported her to the agency. I dare say my husband has not been the only one, and, whilst I cannot fault her care of my children, I would urge you to be on your guard.

It was too late for him to do anything now, of course. Angelina needed Alice too much for him to dismiss her.

Perhaps the relationship had meant more to Alice than Pauline Levinsky knew? Perhaps she had actually loved the other woman's husband? Angrily Marco wondered why on earth he was trying to find excuses for Alice.

Unlike his late cousin, Marco was not a city lover, which was why he had chosen to work from the *palazzo* rather than from a more centrally located office.

Thinking about Aldo made him frown. After his and Patti's death, Marco had driven to Rome in order to collect baby Angelina's things from the apartment where his cousin and his wife had lived.

The baby's cot had been crammed into a tiny room, her few clothes had all been in an untidy heap on the floor, whilst the wardrobes had been crammed with Patti's designer outfits.

Disgusted by what he had found and the apparent lack of concern for Angelina's welfare on the part of her parents he had felt it had revealed, he had gone straight to one of Rome's most exclusive shopping streets, to completely re-equip a nursery and wardrobe for her.

Aldo and Patti had been married less than six months when Aldo had admitted to Marco that Marco had been right to counsel him against marrying so quickly, and that he was now regretting his impulsive actions.

But by then Patti had been pregnant, and Marco had urged Aldo to at least try to make a go of his marriage for the baby's sake.

If he hadn't done so, would both his cousin and Patti still be alive now? Broodingly, Marco acknowledged his own sense of guilt. But no matter how guilty he might feel, there was one person who ought to feel even more so, and that was Angelina's grandmother, Patti's mother, Francine Bailey.

She had been furious when Aldo and Patti had married. Marco had met her for the first time at the party Aldo and Patti had given after their return from honeymoon, when she had told him in no uncertain terms that she wished they had not done so, informing Marco that she had been making plans for Patti to go to Los Angeles, where there had been a producer who had been prepared to offer Patti a part in one of his films.

The moment Marco had been introduced to Francine he had disliked her. In his view it had been a great pity that Francine had not removed her daughter to Los Angeles before she had met his impressionable cousin.

She had made it plain to him at the party that the only virtue she'd been able to see in her daughter's marriage to his cousin was the fact that Marco himself was extremely wealthy.

She was, in Marco's opinion, one of those women who was trying to rewrite the story of her own life through her unfortunate daughter. And Francine had been determined that Patti would fulfil for her her own thwarted dreams of stardom, even if that had meant hothousing her into a vac-

uous blonde bimbo of a girl who'd had 'second rate' written all over her.

Francine had done everything she could to persuade her
daughter to have her pregnancy terminated, and in the end
it had only been Marco's intervention and his promise to
take on full financial responsibility for the little girl in
every single way that had persuaded Patti to go through
with the pregnancy, which was how he had come to be
appointed her temporary guardian.

As he drove out of the city Marco resisted the temptation
to ring the *palazzo* to check how Angelina was. Was that
because he didn't want Alice Walsingham to think he was
checking up on her or because he didn't want to expose
himself to the dangerous pleasure of hearing her voice?

It was too late now for him to acknowledge that she was
too dangerous; too tempting a complication in his life—he
should have known better than to invite her into it.

Right now his prime concern, his only concern, had to
be Angelina and her welfare. Nothing could be allowed to
be more important to him than that, especially not his own
adult desires.

Angelina needed the security of Alice's continued presence in her life in these all-important early years. There
was no way he could allow himself to prejudice that.

And besides, even if he had been foolish enough to feel
some sort of attraction towards her, the Levinsky woman's
letter had surely killed those feelings?

So why was he returning home having cancelled an afternoon meeting he should have been attending?

Why? For Angelina's sake, that was why! Maddalena
had already telephoned him to report Maria's defection—
not that the maid was any real loss—and naturally, as
Angelina's guardian it behoved him to ensure that she was
in the best possible and most caring hands, he assured
himself.

*   *   *

The gardens spread out below the nursery windows looked temptingly beautiful and Alice longed to explore them. Babies in her opinion needed to breathe in fresh air, although here in such a hot climate Angelina would need to be protected from the sun.

She had found a top-of-the-range baby stroller, clearly as yet unused, which had made her frown a little—Angelina was six months old!

Scooping Angelina up and cuddling her, she laughed in delight when Angelina smiled back at her spontaneously and held out her arms to her. Alice dressed her as comfortably as she could.

At least here was one good reason for not trying to get out of having dinner with Marco this evening. She could use the occasion to point out to him that Angelina's wardrobe was in serious need of remodelling. A rueful smile curled her mouth. In a dozen or so years, she doubted that Angelina would be willing to change her designer labels for sensible chain-store clothes! Alice liked timeless, well-designed things herself, but right now she was dressed in a comfortable tee shirt and a soft practical denim skirt. Her contract had specified that she was not to wear a uniform; Marco, it seemed, wanted someone who was more of a surrogate mother to his little girl than a mere nanny.

Having negotiated the stairs with the stroller and finally found her way outside, with albeit some willing help from Maddalena, Alice recognised ruefully that Angelina's head wasn't the only one that should have protection from the strong sun, but unfortunately she had forgotten to bring her own hat down, and there was no way she was going to either go back upstairs with the stroller, or leave Angelina outside on her own.

Protected from the strength of the sun Angelina gurgled happily in her stroller as Alice walked her through the breathtakingly beautiful formal gardens. As she pushed the stroller Alice talked to Angelina, commenting on everything she could see.

'Look, Angelina,' she told her, positioning the stroller so that Angelina could follow the direction in which she was pointing. 'Roses…'

Lifting her out of the stroller, she held her carefully, close to the rose, breathing in its scent herself, rich, musky, sun drenched, laughing as the baby copied her, her eyes opening wide in awe.

'Rose,' Alice repeated, hugging her tightly.

In the distance she could hear water tinkling. Turning to put Angelina back into the stroller, she gave a startled gasp as she realised that they were not on their own and that the doctor had arrived unannounced and was standing watching them.

'What a delightful picture,' he complimented her with old-fashioned charm as he smiled at her. 'I apologise if I startled you. I thought I would call and see how our little one was doing, although I can now see that my visit was unnecessary.'

A little uncomfortably Alice admitted to herself that, whereas she would have instantly resented Marco's unexpected appearance, suspecting that he did not trust her judgement, where the doctor was concerned she felt only gratitude for his professionalism.

'She seems fine, her temperature is down and she's finished all her formula. I'd like to start her on something a little bit more substantial, but I'm a firm believer in babies having only the freshest, organically produced foods.'

'A view with which you will find Marco will concur,' the doctor told her warmly.

'He is a far better father to the little one than—' He broke off exclaiming, 'Ah, here he is himself, so you will be able to address your concerns about Angelina's food to him.'

To her consternation Alice felt her face starting to pinken whilst her heart was pounding so frantically and so erratically that it was no wonder she felt dizzy.

The heat of the garden, which five minutes ago had seemed reasonably bearable, now for some reason made her feel as though she could barely breathe.

Mercifully yesterday's vicious headache had eased, although she was conscious that it was still there, lurking threateningly, and that it was extremely foolish of her not to have covered her unprotected head from the strong heat of the sun.

'Ah, Marco,' the doctor hailed the *conte*, 'I have just been privileged to witness the most delightful scene. Your charming Alice was showing Angelina one of your roses.'

His charming Alice... The doctor was making it sound as though she was...they were...hurriedly, anxious to dismiss her own thoughts, Alice rushed into a husky explanation, 'I believe it is important for even the youngest baby to receive sensory stimulation, of a positive kind, and the perfume of these roses...'

'They were planted by my mother. She loved their scent.'

She really ought not to have come out into the garden without something to cover her head, Alice acknowledged dizzily. The sun was far too strong for her, she was beginning to feel sickly light-headed and she knew that had she been on her own with Angelina she would have sensibly and immediately sought out some shade, or gone back indoors, but her pride would not allow her in Marco's presence to either show any weakness or to admit that she had made even the smallest error of judgement.

Angelina had now seen Marco, and a broad smile had broken out across her small face. Kicking excitedly, she lifted her arms imperiously demanding to be picked up.

A little to Alice's surprise, Marco immediately did so, leaning into the stroller to remove her.

For some reason the way he cradled her against his

shoulder brought a distinct lump of emotion to Alice's throat. He looked the picture of devoted fatherhood.

'It is a real pleasure to see the little one starting to thrive after all she has been through,' the doctor was saying, shaking his head as he continued. 'It is a mercy that she was not in the car.' He stopped, putting his hand on Marco's arm as he exclaimed softly, 'I am sorry, my friend, if I am distressing you. I have not forgotten that you lost someone you loved very deeply in that tragedy.'

Alice could scarcely believe her ears. According to everything she had been told Marco and his wife had been on the point of divorcing, but now here was the doctor implying that Marco had loved her very much. Alice didn't want to dig deeper into the unpleasant feeling that realisation was giving her! It wasn't jealousy, was it? Jealousy of a dead woman because…because what? Don't go there! her instincts warned her protectively.

Suddenly sharply conscious that Marco was watching her, she turned quickly away, and then gasped as the unpleasant physical sensations she had been fighting to keep at bay for the last few minutes abruptly overwhelmed her.

The knowledge that she was about to faint panicked her, her first thought relief that she wasn't holding Angelina, and her second, and last, distress that Marco was going to witness her weakness.

When she came round she was sitting propped up against a tree, sheltered from the sun by its leaves. The doctor was crouching at her side smiling reassuringly at her, whilst Marco was standing grimly to one side watching them both.

Anxiously she looked for Angelina.

'The baby,' she began shakily.

'Safe in her stroller,' the doctor reassured her. 'Marco put her there before he carried you over here. How do you feel? You gave us both quite a shock…'

'I…I…fine,' Alice assured him. 'I think I must have stayed out in the sun too long…'

'I am sure you are right,' the doctor agreed. 'But…' He paused and looked towards Marco.

'I have just informed the doctor about yesterday's accident. It concerns me that you could be suffering from concussion…'

Concussion! Alice looked at him in disbelief.

'I worked in a hospital,' she reminded him. 'And I think I'd know if I had concussion. I'm sure it's nothing more than the heat.'

One dark eyebrow rose in ironic disbelief.

'And I should have thought that with your nursing experience, you would also have known that you were suffering from heatstroke or sunstroke and done something about it, such as wearing a hat,' he pointed out dryly. 'I think it best that you are checked over. The doctor is on his way to our local hospital now and he will drive you there.'

Hospital! Alice stared at them both.

'No, that isn't necessary,' she protested stubbornly. 'I can't go to hospital. Who will look after Angelina?'

'I will look after her,' Marco informed her. 'And as for you not going…as your employer, it is my right and my duty to insist that you do, even if I have to take you there myself,' he warned her with ominously quiet emphasis.

Concussion! This was ridiculous. Alice knew that she had no such thing, and that she was simply suffering from the heat, but she could see that neither of the two men was going to listen to her.

'Marco is right to be concerned,' the doctor told her gently, confirming her private thoughts.

'You may believe that the accident did no damage, but it is best that we check. Unfortunately the symptoms produced by concussion can be similar to those caused by heatstroke, at least in the early stages, and I would be doing less than my duty as a doctor if I did not insist that you allow me to put all our minds at rest.'

Put like that, how could she continue to refuse? Alice admitted. She really had no alternative other than to give in and go with the doctor.

'If you feel well enough to walk to my car,' he began courteously. Out of the corner of her eye Alice could see Marco watching her, frowning.

'Perfectly well enough,' she told him with faked breeziness and assurance. And it wasn't entirely a lie. She fully intended to make sure that she was well enough, even if she had to grit her teeth against a second bout of sickening dizziness when she made to stand up.

She could see Marco's eyes beginning to narrow, but mercifully, before he could make any comment, Angelina started to cry.

All three of them looked towards the stroller instinctively, but it was Alice who started to walk towards it first. However, Marco quickly overtook her, cursing under his breath as he ordered her, 'Keep still. Do you want to faint a second time? I will look after Angelina. Wait here, please, and then I shall escort you to his car, to make sure that you get there safely.'

His high-handedness infuriated Alice; she felt as though he was brushing her impatiently to one side, deriding her skills, questioning her judgement and her professionalism, and before she could stop herself she heard herself demanding scornfully, 'You mean the way you were looking after her before I arrived…leaving her to the mercy of an untrained and even less caring girl, who was virtually half starving her with her ignorance, never mind….'

Horrified, she closed her mouth. Whatever her private opinions might be, she had no right to publicise them. And normally she would not have done so, but there was something about her new employer that got under her skin in a way that no one else she had worked for had ever done.

She was breaking all the rules about keeping a formal

distance between them, behaving in a way that was totally unprofessional, allowing her emotions to run riot and dictate her behaviour. Alice knew but somehow she couldn't stop herself! A quick look over her shoulder reassured her that the doctor was too far away to have heard her, thankfully—but Marco quite plainly had.

'If by that you mean what I think you mean,' he began in a dangerously clipped and quiet voice, 'then let me assure you that I was very much aware of the inadequacy of the care Angelina was receiving, which was why I hired you,' he told her pointedly.

Alice knew that it would be politic for her to seize the opportunity he had given her and back off, letting the subject drop, but to her own consternation she heard herself blurting out almost aggressively, 'She needs more clothes. Those she has are far too formal and impractical. They look as though someone has just gone out and...'

She stopped as she saw the way he was looking at her.

Curtly he told her, 'I had no other option. The things she already had...' He gave a small shrug of distaste. 'Patti was not the best of housewives—or mothers. If in my inexperience I have not provided Angelina with what she needs, then that can soon be rectified. In the meantime, if you will oblige me by going with the doctor.'

Pointedly he stood between Alice and the stroller, waiting until the doctor had come up with them and then telling him, 'We have delayed you enough. Let us get Ms Walsingham safely in your car, so that you can return to the hospital. If you will telephone me once you have the results of the necessary tests?'

It was on the tip of Alice's tongue to say that there was no way she wanted or needed him to check on her health, but caution prevented her from doing so. The last thing she wanted to do right now was to sound even more like a petulant, overwrought child than she no doubt already did.

After they had walked slowly to the doctor's car, and

Alice was just about to get into it, she found herself wishing that she had been allowed to kiss Angelina goodbye, and then, to her astonishment, as though he had somehow guessed what she was thinking, Marco turned and lifted the baby out of the stroller, holding her out to Alice! He really was the most complex man, so arrogantly hard and controlled one minute, and the next seemingly almost to understand her every emotion as keenly as though he were her most intimate companion!

Determinedly ignoring the powerful male arms holding her charge, and the fact that she now smelled not just of baby powder but of expensive male cologne as well, Alice leaned forward and kissed her tenderly on her cheek, whispering lovingly to her as she did so, 'Don't worry, little one, I shall be back soon.'

She was worried, though, and her face crinkled into an anxious frown as she told Marco, 'Who will give her her formula? There is some made up in the fridge, but Maria has left and—'

'I am perfectly capable of giving her her bottle,' Marco assured her wryly. 'It won't be the first time I have done so, I can assure you.'

'You won't try to rush her, will you?' Alice couldn't help herself from asking anxiously. 'Only she does tend to take her time, and—'

'I won't rush her.'

Marco was already turning away from her. Unhappily Alice closed the car door. Marco was her employer and in this instance she had to do as he was demanding, little though she liked it or thought it necessary.

The last thing she thought as the doctor drove away was that at least now she would be spared the ordeal of having dinner with him!

CHAPTER SIX

IN THE solitude of her hospital room, Alice started to get dressed. Just as she had known would be the case, the hospital tests had proved that all she was suffering from was a little too much Italian sun. When the doctor had smilingly given her that news, she had itched for Marco to be there so that she could say, 'I told you so.' But even more than she wanted to do that had she wanted to be back at the *palazzo* with Angelina.

However, when she had suggested as much to the doctor he had informed her that Marco had insisted that she was to remain at the hospital overnight.

'It was just the heat,' Alice had protested, and the doctor had smiled in acknowledgement but had then reminded her, 'When you've witnessed the appalling devastation of a fatal car accident as Marco has done, it is perhaps understandable that he should be anxious to ensure that you have not been injured.'

His gentle reproof had left Alice with no option other than to settle herself ruefully into the private hospital room she had been shown to—at the *conte*'s insistence it was a private room.

And now here she was getting dressed and wondering just how she was going to get back to the *palazzo*. Would Marco send someone to collect her, or would she have to make her own way back? She could hardly expect the doctor, busy man as he obviously was, to drive her.

By some miraculous means she had woken to find that the clothes she had been wearing when she had arrived at the hospital had been laundered for her, and the *en suite* bathroom to her private room had provided everything she could have needed in the way of toiletries.

It was eight o'clock. Had Angelina wondered where she was when she had woken up or had there been so many strangers in and out of her short life that she'd simply accepted her disappearance?

The previous evening Alice had been provided with a menu from which to choose her breakfast, and when she heard the brief rap on her door she assumed that it was now being delivered, but when she called out, 'Come in,' to her consternation and shock it was Marco who opened the door and walked into her room.

Thankful that she was actually dressed, Alice demanded anxiously, 'Where is Angelina? Who is looking after her?'

'She is here with me,' Marco astonished her by answering, going back to the door to wedge it open and wheel in Angelina in her stroller.

To Alice's joy the baby recognised her immediately and smiled at her.

Alice noticed he was dressed in immaculately clean clothes, and it seemed to Alice that she was already looking slightly plumper.

Immediately she went to her, laughing as Angelina held out her arms to her. Unfastening her from the stroller, she picked her up to cuddle her, unselfconsciously crooning lovingly to her, 'Who's a pretty, pretty girl, then? Did you have all your formula? Let me look and see that new tooth you've got coming.'

'You don't need to see it, I can give you a categoric assurance that it has come through,' Marco told her feelingly, indicating a tiny little tooth-mark on his finger.

Alice couldn't help herself, she started to laugh.

'It's no laughing matter,' Marco told her dryly. 'Those teeth are sharp.'

It was only now seeing the baby that Alice acknowledged just how worried she had been about her. She had woken several times during the night worrying about her, and now she couldn't stop herself from beaming her pleasure and relief at seeing her to Marco as she told him guilelessly, 'Thank you for bringing her. I've been so worried about her…'

The bitterness of the look that Marco gave her as she spoke shocked her into silence. What on earth was it she had said that was making him look so angry? Surely as Angelina's primary carer she had every right to be worried about her? Wasn't that after all why he was employing her? Or had his fatherly instinct certainly become activated, and was he perhaps jealous that Angelina might become too attached to her?

Angrily Marco wondered just what it was about Alice that made it so easy for her to tug on his heartstrings. Never in the admittedly brief time Patti had been alive had he ever once heard her express the slightest degree of concern about her baby, and yet here was Alice, who had barely known her a full twenty-four hours, exhibiting intense anxiety about her.

Which was why he'd employed her, he reminded himself, sternly. And the only reason why.

Just as the only reason he was here right now instead of sending someone to collect Alice was because of Angelina!

'You mentioned yesterday that Angelina needed some clothes, so I thought, since the good doctor has declared you to be fit and well, that we could go to Florence this morning and you could pick out yourself exactly what you think is needed.'

Had she actually been foolish enough to think he had come to collect her for some personal reason?

If so she had learned a painful lesson, Alice derided herself. And anyway, she challenged her emotions, why should she care? He meant nothing to her. She didn't even like him.

Who had mentioned anything as simple as 'liking him'? a taunting inner voice mocked her unkindly.

An hour later, shaking her head in rejection of yet another designer babywear shop, its windows decorated with the most beautiful and impractical of outfits, Alice felt her heart begin to sink—in more ways than one. All the other women shopping in the expensive street were obviously Italian and equally obviously stunningly well dressed, and she was beginning to feel acutely self-conscious in her clean but rather basic outfit. Marco, of course, was immaculately dressed, father and daughter very obviously a pair, whilst she, she suspected, must equally obviously look an outsider.

'We shall have to go back to the *palazzo* soon,' she informed Marco warningly. 'Angelina will be due for another feed.'

'I know. I brought a couple of bottles of her formula with me. They're here,' he told Alice, lightly tapping the bag attached to the stroller.

Alice tried not to look as uncomposed as she felt at this usurpation of her role. It was on the tip of her tongue to question just how he had made the formula, but somehow she managed to stop herself. Angelina was Marco's daughter, she reminded herself, and she ought to be pleased that he was being so responsible instead of feeling pushed out and unnecessary.

'I thought we'd give it another half an hour and then take a break,' Marco was saying. 'There's an excellent hotel not far from here—I know the owner.'

He would do, of course, Alice found herself thinking ruefully as they turned a corner and walked straight into a busy, bustling street market.

Her eyes shining with mischief she announced to Marco, tongue in cheek, 'Now, this is much better. I'm sure we can find the sort of things Angelina needs here.'

To her surprise, instead of immediately refusing to take

another step, Marco actually nodded and started to walk in the direction of the first stall.

The street was a seething mass of people, the stalls awash with 'factory price' leather goods, coats, shoes, and designer bags of spurious parentage and of course the ever-present tee-shirt stalls.

The crowds seething through the narrow street were a mixture of bargain-hunting tourists, guides trying to shepherd their distracted sightseeing flocks, and even a fair smattering of elegantly and expensively well-heeled dedicated shoppers, but as Alice made to join them she felt Marco's restraining hand on her arm.

Enquiringly she turned to look at him, expecting to hear him express disdain for the market and insist that they shop elsewhere, but instead and to her confusion he told her firmly, 'These places are fun, I know, but please stay close to me. There will be pickpockets around. And I should hate you to be the victim of a theft.'

He was concerned for her! As she listened to him Alice could feel the heat of his touch burning against her skin. It shocked her that she should feel so acutely aware of him…far too acutely aware and in far, far too dangerous a way. The surge of the crowds threw her slightly off balance so that she fell against him. Immediately alarmed by the reaction of her own body to him, she tried to pull back. But it was too late, She had already started to overbalance, and he had of course reacted instantly and reached out to steady her with both hands. The jostling of the crowd had brought her up so close to him that her breasts were flat against his chest. One of his hands had dropped to her hip. She could feel herself starting to tremble as she realised that her lower body was resting against the hard warmth of his thigh.

She was aware of him with every pore of her skin, every part of her sensory system; she was aware of him in a thousand unwanted and alarming ways. She was aware of him with an intensity that shocked her and was totally outside her experience.

'Angelina,' she managed to remind him as she pulled herself away from him. She knew that her face was flushed and hoped that he would put it down to the heat of the sun. And that open, urgent peaking of her nipples? Would he put that down to the heat of the sun as well, or would he guess that it was caused by a heat of a very, very different nature?

Quickly she started to walk down the street, only to have to stop when Marco called out, 'Wait.'

As his hand snaked out to grasp her upper arm Alice willed herself not to allow that deep, intense quiver that had begun low down in her body, and which was threatening to spread to every single one of her nerve endings, to betray her even further by causing her whole body to shiver in sensual overreaction.

'This way,' Marco commanded, drawing her towards one of the stalls.

At first Alice thought he must have seen a babywear stall, but to her astonishment the stall he was leading her to sold, not babywear, but the most exquisite and obviously handmade straw hats.

'You need one of these,' he told her firmly. 'Then you will be able to keep your head covered from the sun.'

'Yes, I do,' Alice agreed uncertainly. She had already given the hats a quick glance and had seen immediately from the price that these were no cheap holiday items.

As though she had guessed what she was thinking, the stallholder immediately began to tell Alice in English, 'These hats, they are from one of Italy's most famous designers. She has a factory not far from here, and these are...'

As she fought for the right word Alice supplied for her in English, 'Seconds,' and then translated the word into Italian for her, earning herself a wryly impressed look from the other woman.

'You speak Italian?' she questioned Alice.

'Yes,' Alice confirmed. 'And these hats, whilst they are lovely, are far too expensive for me, I'm afraid.'

'But, no, they are a bargain,' the woman insisted. 'Try this one. It will be perfect for you, and I promise you it will be worth its cost.'

Before Alice could stop her, she was firmly placing one of the hats on Alice's head. A soft, natural-coloured straw, it felt as soft and as supple as fabric, and as Alice peeped into the mirror she was holding up for her she was forced to admit that both the style and the colour did suit her.

'The hat is possible to be folded,' the woman began to explain, and then with a small shrug switched to Italian as she told Alice that the hat was designed to be folded away, and that it was virtually the last one she had of a very special range.

Alice began to shake her head, but suddenly to her consternation she heard Marco saying firmly, 'We will take it.'

He was already handing over the money, whilst the stall-holder, emboldened by her success, was attempting to persuade him that Angelina too needed a hat, 'To match her mama's,' she announced.

Her mama's! Alice looked away from her and then wished she hadn't as her gaze immediately meshed with Marco's.

What was it that was making her heart ache in that darkly dangerous way? A secret wish that Angelina, whom she had already come to love so deeply, was her child, or an even more secret wish that Marco had sired her baby? What on earth was she thinking? That heatstroke must have been far more potent than she had realised! There was no way she intended to allow such thoughts to flourish! No way!

As they left the stall Alice started to open her bag to find the money with which to repay Marco.

'What are you doing?' he demanded when he saw her.

When Alice told him, he stopped walking and frowned.

'The hat is a…a necessary item of your wardrobe whilst you are working for me and as such it is my desire to pay for it!' he told her coolly.

'No. I can't let you do that!' Alice protested.

'You can't stop me,' Marco informed her, touching her arm before she could say anything else to tell her, 'There is a shop over there that has baby clothes.'

Distracted, Alice turned to look in the direction he was pointing.

Five minutes later, standing inside the shop she was nodding in happy approval of the outfits its owner was showing her.

'These are exactly the sorts of things she needs,' she told Marco enthusiastically.

'Fine. Get whatever you think she needs,' he responded.

Carefully Alice chose several outfits, shaking her head when Marco picked up one item, and telling him determinedly, 'No, that colour does not suit her.'

The smile that curled his mouth along with the tender look that accompanied it caught her off guard. They were, she told herself forcefully, for Angelina and most certainly not for her. How could they be?

'Are you sure that's enough?' Marco questioned her when she had finished.

'She'll be growing out of them so quickly, it's silly to get too many,' Alice informed him.

Angelina, who had been asleep, had started to wake up, and experience told Alice that she would soon be feeling very hungry.

'If that hotel you mentioned isn't too far away,' she began as Marco paid for their purchases, 'I think it might be a good idea to make our way there.'

As soon as she heard Alice's voice, Angelina turned to look at her, grizzling to be picked up and cuddled.

Only too happy to respond, Alice removed her from the

stroller for a cuddle as she told her, 'Formula time soon, honeybun…'

She had spoken to her automatically in Italian and the shop owner laughed, and joined in the conversation, informing Alice that she had a grandson of Angelina's age.

Angelina, wide awake now, started to exercise her new tooth on the exposed curve of Alice's neck.

'Oh, no, you don't, young lady,' Marco informed Angelina firmly as he saw what she was doing, and reached out to lift her out of Alice's arms to put her back in the stroller.

As they left the shop Alice couldn't help wondering how they had looked to the shop owner. Had she guessed that Alice was simply Angelina's nanny or had she believed that she was her child; that she and Marco were a couple?

Aghast by the direction her thoughts were taking, Alice brought them to a frantic, skidding halt.

What she was doing was crazy, idiotic, self-destructive and downright foolish. It was bad enough that she had fallen in love with Angelina, without her falling in love with her father as well!

Falling in love with Marco? Her? No, that was totally impossible! When she fell in love it would be with a man she could feel comfortable and relaxed with, not a too-sexy, too-arrogant man with one apparently bad marriage behind him, and an attitude toward his baby that…

But what exactly was Marco's attitude towards Angelina? Right now he was interacting with her as though parenting came as naturally to him as breathing.

'It's this way.'

Realising that Marco was waiting for her to cross the road with him, she shook herself free of her unwanted and disturbing thoughts and feelings.

As they walked into the foyer of a breathtakingly elegant private hotel a few minutes later, she realised she was attracting more than one interested and approving look from the men they had walked past.

Without really realising what she was doing she instinctively moved a little bit closer to Marco and the stroller. She could see he was frowning. Because he didn't want her so close to him? He hadn't made any move away from her, though, and in fact he reached out to place his hand on her shoulder as he pointed out a secluded table to her where they could sit and have coffee and still look out onto the busy street, with its distant view of the river.

'We'll need to ask them to heat up Angelina's bottle,' she warned him. 'And I'd like to change her.'

Escorting her to the table he had indicated, Marco inclined his head.

'Leave everything to me,' he told her, before asking, 'Would you like to have a cup of coffee before we order lunch?'

'Coffee would be lovely,' Alice agreed, busying herself moving Angelina's stroller so that the baby was tucked safely between her own chair and the window.

Alice was talking softly to Angelina, the baby's eyes fixed adoringly on her face, when Marco returned. He paused for a second watching them, his mouth twisting in wry acknowledgement of what he could no longer hide from himself. It was a pity that their children would be unlikely to inherit her blonde hair, and he wasn't sure whether or not he wanted their daughters to inherit their mother's dangerously sexy soft pink mouth. If they did, they would no doubt grow up tormenting every man who saw them in exactly the same way their mother was tormenting him right now...

Alice turned her head and looked at him. His heart slammed heavily against his ribs as he looked back at her.

Alice felt her heart miss a beat and then flutter frantically against her chest. Why was Marco looking at her like that...as though...as though...?

'I've had a word with the hotel manager, and he has put a room at our disposal where you may take Angelina when you are ready.'

Alice tried not to look impressed.

'I've also ordered our coffee,' Marco told her, pulling out a chair to sit down next to her.

As he leaned over to smile at Angelina his thigh brushed against Alice's.

The minute shudder that ran through her was immediate and unstoppable. The images forming in her mind were so sensual and so explicit that they shocked her. Shocked her and excited her, she acknowledged shakily. She had never felt so sexually aware of any man, so sexually aware of him and so sexually hungry for him!

How on earth had it happened? One moment she had disliked and despised him and the next, or so it seemed now, her body was a tormenting ache of sensual female need for his touch, for his mouth, for him!

Their coffee arrived, but Alice was oblivious to the admiring look the young waiter gave her, her eyes darkening with the intensity of the painful inward delving of her thoughts. How could this unwanted transformation of her emotions have taken place? That she should virtually immediately have felt love for Angelina was, so far as she was concerned, perfectly understandable, the baby was after all crying out for her to give and receive human love, but where on earth had her foolish heart got the idea that her father either needed or would reciprocate her love?

'Your coffee's getting cold.'

The crisp, almost critical note in Marco's voice made her realise how quickly she had become sensitive to every changing timbre of it.

'Angelina will be wanting her bottle,' she informed him shakily.

'Give it to me,' Marco instructed her. He summoned a waiter, to whom he handed the bottle Alice had removed from the bag, asking him to arrange for it to be warmed, at the same time also asking him to bring them some lunch menus.

'Everything here is freshly prepared and cooked,' he

told Alice once they had their menus. 'The pasta with beef is a speciality of the restaurant and I can recommend it. Or if you would prefer fish…'

'No, the beef sounds delicious,' Alice assured him, turning to smile at the waiter as he returned with Angelina's bottle.

Lifting the baby out of her stroller, she settled her comfortably in her arm, smiling at her as she began to feed her.

'She's already eating much better,' she told Marco enthusiastically. 'Babies are so sensitive to the emotions of people around them—she must be missing her mother so dreadfully,' she added, her voice faltering as she realised that Marco too might be missing the woman who had been his wife and the mother of his child. It was all very well for Maddalena to say that the marriage had not been a happy one, but that did not mean….

'Missing her! I don't think so,' Marco countered Alice's comment immediately, his voice harshly grating and so full of suppressed anger that it made Alice want to flinch.

'Patti never wanted Angelina, and once she was born she spent as little time with her as she could. She even insisted on having her delivered by Caesarean section before her actual birth date because she didn't want to miss some shallow social event she wanted to attend!'

Alice could hear the disgust quite openly in his voice.

No, there was quite definitely no love there in his voice for his dead wife, Alice acknowledged.

For some reason her eyes had started to mist with emotional tears. Blinking them away, she brushed her fingertip gently over Angelina's rosebud cheek as the baby clung to her bottle.

'She is so lovely, so precious. I cannot…' she began, and then had to stop as her emotions suspended her voice. There were some things it was neither right nor fair for her to say, especially about a dead woman who was not there to defend herself. Marco, after all, was her employer and…so far as he knew Alice was the woman who had attempted to steal his car and drive off in it.

It still bemused her that he had actually wanted to employ her knowing that, although she could at least understand now just why he had been so desperate to get a proper nanny for Angelina.

Their lunch arrived just as Angelina finished her bottle.

Putting her back in her stroller, Alice saw the waiter filling her wineglass and her eyes widened.

She didn't normally drink at lunchtime, but it seemed churlish to make a fuss, and the wine was deliciously smooth on the palate, she acknowledged as she took a small, tentative sip.

Like the French, Italians knew how to enjoy their food and make even the simplest meal an occasion.

All the tables around them had filled up, some with business-suited men, others with smart middle-aged women carrying glossy shopping bags with discreet designer logos and others with family groups, and a cheerful, happy buzz of chatter filled the room.

A young mother at an adjacent table smiled conspiratorially towards Alice as she saw Angelina. Her own two toddlers were immaculately dressed and plainly at home in such an adult environment.

'No, really, I couldn't,' Alice protested, refusing a final cappuccino. She had already eaten a full plate of pasta and beef, plus a deliciously wicked tiramisu ice cream, plus a large glass of rich red wine, and it was no wonder that she was feeling so wonderfully relaxed.

Not so relaxed, though, that she had forgotten her responsibilities.

'I'd better take Angelina upstairs to change her now,' she told Marco.

'Very well.'

As she stood up so did he, helping her to manoeuvre

the stroller into a clear space, and then pushing it into the foyer and towards the bank of lifts.

'We're on the fourth floor,' he informed Alice as he pressed the button.

Nodding absently, Alice waited until the lift doors opened and then stepped out.

'This way,' Marco instructed her, pushing the stroller with one hand whilst he removed an old-fashioned room key from his pocket with the other.

'This hotel was originally a private home,' he explained to Alice as he paused outside one of the heavy doors and inserted the key into the lock.

'During the conversion as many of the original features as possible were retained.'

'It is very beautiful,' Alice agreed, casting an admiring look down the corridor with its frescoed walls and ornately plastered ceiling.

Pushing open the bedroom door, Marco waited for her to go inside.

The room was huge, dominated by an enormous king-sized bed. Through its balcony windows Alice could see the river.

'I'll take Angelina through to the bathroom,' she told Marco as she lifted her out of the stroller. For some reason she had not expected him to accompany them to the room, and now for no logical reason she could think of she felt thoroughly unnerved by his presence and acutely aware of it—and of him. For no logical reason maybe, but she certainly emotionally knew exactly why she was reacting to him the way she was. Exactly why!

The bathroom was as generously proportioned as the bedroom, and fitted with gleaming white sanitary-ware.

Through the half-open door Alice was aware of Marco making a call on his mobile as she deftly undressed Angelina and started to change her. She had brought the changing bag attached to the stroller into the bathroom with her, with everything that she needed.

Marco was speaking into his mobile, and Alice tensed as she heard him asking how long it was going to be before the Ferrari was ready for collection.

Kissing Angelina's clean, bare skin, she started to re-dress her.

'You are so delicious, I could eat you,' she cooed to the baby, tenderly.

Marco listened to her. What was it about this woman that made her so instinctively, and so damn sexily, maternal? The way she made him feel right now meant that just to hear her, never mind look at her, made him ache in an entirely male and driven way to ensure that it was his children she would be mothering.

The words he could hear her murmuring to Angelina were only a mild echo of his own far more elemental and tormenting longing to say the same thing to Alice, and not just to say it, he acknowledged grimly as he listened to the garage's service manager explaining to him that the Ferrari was almost ready for collection.

Marco tensed as he saw Alice coming out of the bathroom, carrying Angelina.

'I think she's ready to go back down now,' she told him as she walked towards the stroller.

As she reached him Angelina turned in her arms, nuzzling toward Alice's breast. Marco knew it was an automatic baby reaction, and equally automatic was his own body's reaction to it, to them. Angelina might not be his child, but he felt as though she were. He loved her as though she were, and the sight of Alice gently giving her her finger to suck as she tenderly placed her in her stroller did things to his senses he would have sworn to be impossible before she had come into his life.

Within seconds of her putting Angelina in her stroller, she was fast asleep. Smiling, Alice stepped back from her and then gave a small gasp of shock as she came up against something solid.

She hadn't realised that Marco was standing behind her. Automatically she started to turn round and then wished she hadn't as she realised that Marco hadn't moved and that now they were standing body to body, and that hers was resting on him in a way that meant it must be impossible for him not to realise just how physically aware of him she was!

She could feel the air in the room prickling against her skin, her nerve endings felt so sensitive. She wished she were anywhere but here; she wished he were a thousand miles away and at the same time she wished he were a thousand millimetres closer. She wanted....

'Why are you looking at me like that?' she demanded shakily, saying the first thing that came into her head. 'If it's because of your car, I can pay for the repairs,' she told him, her head lifting proudly.

'To hell with the Ferrari,' Marco responded to her forcefully, shocking her with the intensity of his reaction. 'This has nothing to do with any damned car.'

Emotions seemed to crackle like lightning between them, but stubbornly Alice refused to give in to them.

'Then what, why...?' Alice's voice cracked nervously as she tried to move away, but Marco had placed a restraining hand on her arm, and now its palm was cupping the ball of her shoulder, and not just cupping it but also actually massaging it...

Unable to stop herself, Alice closed her eyes, swaying giddily. This just could not be happening; that message of sexually charged urgency she was getting from his touch just couldn't be real.

Helplessly she looked up at him. Just the sight of his mouth made her feel weak and dizzy. She wanted to reach out and trace the shape of it, with her fingertip, her lips, her tongue.

She could feel her whole body reacting to him, aching for him!

As though it were happening in slow motion she

watched the downward descent of his head, his mouth coming towards her own, felt her heart slamming against her chest wall, her body shuddering from head to toe as he slid his hand beneath her hair, cupping the back of her neck, his thumb stroking the soft, sensitive skin behind her ear.

She could hear the soft, sighing half-moan, half-purr of pleasure she was making as though the sound were coming from somewhere else, her lips already parting in moist eagerness, her eyes heavy and sultry with longing as she semiswooned against him, her body drenched with sensual hunger.

The touch of his mouth on her own, instead of satisfying her need, only seemed to heighten and intensify it. Without knowing what she was doing she found that she was clinging to him, her body pressed tightly into his, desperately seeking its maleness as though it needed him to complete it; as though she needed him to complete her.

His tongue brushed her lips, rough, warm velvet mixed with pure, sensual silk, a thousand unbelievable sensations condensed into one tantalisingly brief touch. Immediately her mouth clung to his wanting more, her own tongue darting boldly against his seeking the intimacy she craved.

His hand touched her breast, and immediately she ached to be naked against him, to feel his touch against her bare skin.

As though he had read her mind, he pushed aside her top, his hand dark against the white fabric of her bra. Her whole body quivered as he pulled the fabric away from her breast, her flesh softly pale against the masculine darkness of his. Unable to stop herself Alice started to moan, gasping for breath as she did so.

His thumb rubbed slowly against the hard nub of her nipple and she cried out in helpless longing, desperate for the feel of his mouth where his thumb had been, ready to offer herself up to her desire for him. Marco was everything she wanted.

She cried out in shocked arousal as he dropped to his knees in front of her and started to kiss the exposed flesh above the waistband of her skirt, slowly moving upwards as he pushed up her tee shirt.

Her entire body was trembling with aching longing as his mouth moved closer to her breast... Another minute, another few seconds of the tormenting, achingly teasing, unbearable, erotic little kisses and his mouth would be on her breast and he would...

The sudden sharp cry that Angelina gave burst through the private bubble of their mutual desire, fracturing it, bringing them both into frozen stillness, even the previous sensual heaviness of their breathing suspended as they both looked towards the stroller.

It was Alice who broke away first, though, tugging down her tee shirt, her face hot with self-conscious embarrassment and disbelief at the way she had been behaving as she hurried over to the baby.

Picking her up, she walked over to the window with her, comforting her, and glad of the excuse not to have to turn round and face Marco. What was he thinking? Was he as shocked by what had happened as she now was, or was he cynically used to foolish young women throwing themselves at him...wanting him...?

Alice cringed as she realised what she had done. He was her employer, a newly bereaved man...a father...and if his sexual needs had overwhelmed him, well, no one would blame him for them having done so, but people would view her behaviour in a very different light. Unfair, but true nonetheless, Alice acknowledged as she tried to recover her composure, telling Marco without turning round, 'I'll take Angelina back downstairs...'

There was no point in her trying to pretend to herself any longer; somehow or other she had been idiotic enough to fall in love with Marco!

* * *

Grimly Marco watched as Alice put Angelina back into the stroller, carefully keeping her back to him.

How the hell had he managed to allow things to get so out of control? After all, it wasn't as though he didn't know exactly what she was under that damnably convincing mask of madonna-like innocent sensuality. She'd had an affair with a married man! Maybe more than one! That kind of behaviour was totally abhorrent to him! Well, there was no way it could be allowed to happen again! He was forced to concede that it had shocked him to discover just how strong his desire for Alice was. A sign that he had lived a celibate life for too long, no doubt! Was she perhaps thinking that he could fill the place left empty in her life by her ex-lover…the place left empty in her bed?

Before he shared his bed with a woman he needed to know his relationship with her was exclusive—and committed; emotionally as well as sexually.

No doubt to a woman like Alice such old-fashioned ideals would simply be amusing; something she simply could not comprehend!

What on earth was she doing? What was happening to her? Alice wondered wretchedly. She had heard of nannies falling into the trap of becoming emotionally and sexually involved with their male employers, but she had never imagined it could ever happen to her! She had always considered herself to be far too sensible.

CHAPTER SEVEN

'I'LL bring Angelina in.'

Nodding, Alice got out of Marco's car. They had travelled back from Florence virtually in silence, and despite the air-conditioning inside the car she had felt stifled and barely able to breathe, as though somehow the sheer weight and burden of her own emotions were sucking the energy and life-giving oxygen out of the air around her.

As she hurried towards the *palazzo*, she was acutely conscious of Marco striding ahead of her pushing the stroller, an action that in another man would no doubt have made him look as domesticated and safe as a big, soft, neutered cat, but that in Marco only had the unnerving effect of actually emphasising his sexuality. No sexually tamed fireside cat this one. Oh, no, he was all lean, dangerous, predatory, feral, hunting male.

The moment they stepped in the cool hallway of the *palazzo*, Maddalena came hurrying towards them, as though she had been anxiously awaiting their return.

'*Conte*, she began with unusual formality, 'there is someone—'

'So at last,' a harsh woman's voice began. 'I have been waiting virtually all day to see my granddaughter, and this...this creature has totally refused to so much as allow me even a glass of water. But then I suppose I should not have expected anything else. After all, like master like servant.'

Alice gasped, instinctively taking a step back from the woman who had erupted into the hallway.

She was tall and bone-thin, dressed in clothes that, whilst obviously expensively high fashion, were openly far too young for her. The skin of her face was pulled so tightly against her bones that Alice wondered that any surgeon with a reputation to worry about could have performed such easily detectable surgery. She fixed Marco with a fulminating glare, totally ignoring Alice's presence as she demanded theatrically, 'Where is my darling precious little girl's baby? Where is she? You have no right to withhold her from me—'

'Calm down, Francine.'

Alice could hear the icy distaste in Marco's voice as he interrupted her emotional tirade.

'Calm down! My daughter is dead, thanks to the dangerous driving of your precious cousin, and now you are trying to steal her child from me. I won't allow you to get away with it, Marco. I am sure the courts will support my claim that her place is with me. After all, I have a blood tie with her that is far stronger than yours. You are only her second cousin, whilst I am her grandmother,' she announced triumphantly, whilst Alice stared at her in bewilderment.

What on earth was she saying? Marco was Angelina's father, surely?

'You may, as you say, have a closer blood tie with Angelina than I do,' Marco was agreeing, totally confounding Alice, 'but her father Aldo appointed me as her guardian.'

'You make me sick,' the woman he had addressed as Francine threw furiously at him. 'Aldo never wanted the baby.'

'Maybe not,' Marco agreed coolly, 'but then neither did your daughter, and as I remember it you were the one who counselled her to have her pregnancy terminated, and even though Aldo had not planned to become a father, he refused to countenance a termination.'

'She had been offered a movie contract.'

Alice could see the grim compression informing Marco's expression as he listened to her bitter response, and she could hear too the suppressed anger in his voice as he told Francine savagely, 'If you think for one minute there is any way I would allow you to have any contact with or influence over Angelina after the way you controlled and ruined your own daughter's life for your own selfish reasons, then you are very, very wrong.'

'What are you saying?' Francine demanded in a high-pitched voice. 'I did everything for Patti. Everything! Sent her to dancing classes, went to auditions with her, paid for her breast implants. Everything. I was the one who helped and encouraged her, who—'

'Who helped and encouraged her to do what?' Marco interrupted her sharply. 'To model semi nude on the pages of a downmarket tabloid. If that is true mother love, then…. There is no way you are going to play any part in Angelina's life, Francine, and as for your coming here and pretending concern for her—don't think I haven't forgotten that you couldn't even be bothered to attend the funeral of the daughter you claim to have loved so much!'

'That was because I couldn't bear the thought of my beautiful baby being buried. Because I was too ill to be there… She was everything to me. And now I want to bring up her daughter…my granddaughter,' she told him triumphantly. 'Angelina is a girl baby. She needs a mother's influence, a female presence in her life. You may be her guardian, but I am her closest next of kin. She needs me in her life,' she told him, with what to Alice seemed to be sickeningly false piety. 'Maria has already been in touch with me to tell me how concerned she has been for her. How you left her knowing she was ill, and refused to call a doctor until Maria begged you to do so. She says you've dismissed her, the very person her mother chose to look after her, and apparently now you've appointed a new nanny to look after her. It's obvious how little you care about her!'

'What? No way is that the truth…'

Marco had gone white with the intensity of his fury and

Alice couldn't blame him. She was still dizzily trying to come to terms with the fact that he was not Angelina's father. Not her father and yet his love for her was shiningly apparent.

'A man cannot bring up a little girl properly,' Francine went on, 'not when she is not his child, and I doubt that any court would actually allow you to do so. There are...' She paused delicately. 'There are certain potential moral issues to be considered...'

The look in Marco's eyes now was positively murderous, and Alice couldn't blame him.

'If you're trying to imply what I think you're trying to imply,' he began ominously, 'then let me tell you—'

'No, Marco, let me tell you that I want Angelina and I intend to have her. And there is no way that you can stop me.' She paused and then said softly, 'I must say I was rather surprised to learn just how wealthy a young man Aldo had been. After all, he kept my poor darling Patti very short of money. That's so very naughty of him when it now turns out that he was close to being a millionaire.'

'So that's it,' Marco commented grimly. 'I might have known! Well, for your information Aldo's inheritance was actually held in trust for him, and unavailable for him to break into it.'

'But it now belongs to Angelina?'

The greedy look in her eyes, which Francine was making no attempt to conceal, sickened Alice. No wonder Marco wanted to protect Angelina from her grandmother. In his shoes Alice would have felt exactly the same.

'In theory, yes, although she will not be able to draw on the capital until she is of age.'

The cool but still calmly good-mannered way in which Marco was answering Francine's questions made Alice marvel at his self-restraint.

'No, of course not. But as her grandmother no doubt I shall be able to make use of the income for necessary expenses for her,' Francine told him with open smugness.

Giving Marco a smile of triumph, she turned to Alice, eyeing her assessingly, with ice-cold, unfriendly eyes.

'You must be the new nanny. Poor Angelina.' She gave a theatrical sigh. 'She must be missing Maria dreadfully. I'm going up to my room now, Marco. Please have something light sent up to me, will you? I refuse to even try to talk to this appalling housekeeper of yours. And you, Nanny—you may bring my granddaughter to me…er… once she has been fed and changed.'

Turning on her heel, she headed towards the stairs, her exit almost as dramatic as her appearance.

Weakly Alice looked at Marco. Now she realised what Maddalena might have meant when she had told her that neither of Angelina's parents had been truly worthy of her.

'Angelina needs her feed,' she told Marco huskily.

Fortunately the baby had slept through the altercation and was only just waking up, her gaze fixed trustingly and lovingly on Alice's face.

'I'll come up with you,' Marco announced abruptly. 'There is something I wish to discuss with you.'

As she lifted Angelina out of the stroller Alice's heart sank. Please don't let him bring up what happened this afternoon! she begged silently as he followed her with the stroller.

The nursery felt welcoming safe and familiar. Alice went to put Angelina in her cot, but Marco stopped her, saying, 'No. Give her to me.'

She must have been blind to have ever believed that he did not love the baby, Alice acknowledged as she saw the look he gave her.

The innate honesty that was so strongly a part of her nature forced her to admit uncomfortably to him, 'I hadn't realised that you were not Angelina's father…'

'You thought she was my child?'

He looked astonished.

'She looks like you,' Alice defended herself, 'and whilst the agency had informed me that she had lost her mother in tragic circumstances they had not said that...' She bit her lip, her voice stumbling to a halt as she saw the look of naked anguish in his eyes.

'Aldo was my cousin, my younger cousin, and we were as close in many ways as though we were brothers. We both lost our parents in the same accident.' He paused, his expression so bleak that Alice ached to be able to say something to comfort him, but how could she? What right did she have to do so?

'I have to admit that Aldo was perhaps a rather spoiled young man. I counselled him not to marry Patti, they were too different!' He paused, his expression grim. 'But Aldo was a very headstrong young man. They had very different aspirations, but neither of them were prepared to listen to any voice of reason or caution; they had fallen in love... Or so they claimed.'

'But you did not consider that to be important,' Alice heard herself challenging him sharply.

She refused to be quelled by the frowning look he was giving her.

'I didn't say that. Love is always important...but their interpretation of love would not be mine, and if it was "love" then I regret to say it was a love of only a very short-lived duration, although it gave me no pleasure when Aldo confirmed that my prediction that this would be the case had proved to be correct. By then Angelina was on the way...'

At the mention of Angelina, Alice put her anger to one side.

'Did her mother really consider terminating her pregnancy?' she couldn't help asking in shock.

'Patti was very much influenced by her mother, and you can see what kind of woman Francine is,' Marco replied.

'What's going to happen? Will she be able to take Angelina away from you?' Alice asked him uncertainly.

'Not whilst I have breath left in my body to prevent it,' Marco assured her vehemently.

'But she does have a…a legitimate claim on her,' Alice pressed him anxiously.

Was she imagining that slight betraying pause before he answered her? That barely discernible hesitation and skilfully covered concern?

'In so far as she is her grandmother, where as I was never legally appointed Angelina's guardian, I'm afraid so, yes,' Marco acknowledged.

'I am a single man with no experience of bringing up a child, and there are those…' He paused, his eyes bleak. 'I am afraid that in the world we live in today, it is necessary for every caring adult to question the motivation of a man bringing up a child who is not his own in a way that it is not with a woman.'

Alice silently digested what he was saying. She knew, of course, what he didn't want to put into words. And she also knew who was the best person to protect Angelina.

'Francine is an instinctive actress and she is very adept at concealing her real personality when the occasion demands it. One hint from her that I might have hidden motives in keeping Angelina with me, and no right-thinking court or judge would want to take that kind of risk.'

Alice could feel her heart starting to beat faster with increasing dread.

'Surely there must be something you can do…some way…?' Alice began, pausing and shaking her head as she told him huskily, 'You can't mean to let her take Angelina.'

There was no doubt in her mind just where Angelina's best interests lay and it certainly wasn't with her grandmother, whom Alice had immediately disliked and distrusted.

Although he was not betraying it, inwardly Marco was fighting the same emotional turmoil as Alice.

Agitatedly she waited for Marco's reply, but then Alice couldn't help saying her thoughts aloud. 'If only you were married. Then surely she couldn't do anything!'

Marco tensed and stared at her. She was right, of course. If he had a wife, then there was no way that Francine could try to claim that he might have some unspeakable ulterior motive in keeping Angelina with him.

'No,' he agreed softly, fixing his gaze on Alice. 'She couldn't.'

Something about the way Marco was looking at her made Alice's heart start to pound frantically fast.

'What…? What is it?' she asked him uncertainly.

'I think you have just given me the answer to my problem.' Marco applauded her. 'I should have seen it for myself,' he continued, more as though he was talking to himself than her, Alice reflected as she waited nervously.

'I thought that in providing Angelina with a nanny who would guarantee to stay with her for a specific length of time that I was doing the very best I could for her, but now I realise that my thinking was not far-sighted enough. What Angelina needs to protect her now is not a nanny, but a woman who would have far more authority in her life in the eyes of the world. What Angelina needs is a mother, a woman who loves her and who has a legal title to prove her right to play the role of mother in her life, and I can think of no one who could fill that role for her better than you, Alice.'

Alice felt as though she wanted to sit down. Her head was spinning, her legs felt weak, and her heart was thudding so heavily that she felt the shock waves of it reverberating right through her body.

Her lips had gone painfully dry, and she was forced to moisten them with the tip of her tongue before she could reply, her body shaking as she saw the way that Marco's gaze homed in on that tiny betraying gesture of nervousness.

'What…what are you trying to say?' she asked him, but she suspected that she already knew what his answer was going to be.

'In order to protect Angelina from Francine I need a

wife—you have said so yourself! Under the circumstances, who better to be that wife, than you?'

'What?' Even though she had been half expecting it, Alice was still gripped by shock. 'No,' she whispered. 'We can't. I can't.'

'Yes, we can. We have to,' Marco insisted fiercely. 'For Angelina's sake.'

If she had still harboured any fugitive thoughts about Marco's love for or commitment to Angelina, what she was hearing and seeing now would have totally put them to flight, Alice recognised.

Here was a man who was totally dedicated to protecting the child fate had placed in his care, even to the extent of marrying a woman he did not love, in order to do so.

She loved Angelina too; could she do any less?

'Think about it,' Marco demanded insistently. 'The more I do, the more sense it makes.'

'I know what you're saying,' Alice was forced to agree, 'but...but marriage?'

Her face had gone pale and Marco could guess what she was thinking.

'So far as you and I are concerned, it will simply be a business arrangement,' he told her calmly. 'A business arrangement, which can be ended after a period of, say, five years, whenever you choose, just as your existing contract can be. I suspect that by that time Francine will have lost interest and found someone else to fasten her greedy talons into, preferably a rich film producer who will keep her safely in Los Angeles,' he added wryly. 'And Angelina will be at school.'

'No, it...it's impossible,' Alice repeated weakly, but she knew that her voice lacked the conviction it should have held. The trouble was that there were issues here that had nothing to do with the 'business arrangement' he was discussing so calmly.

'Why?' Marco was challenging her. 'You have already signed a contract agreeing to remain with Angelina until she goes to school. In agreeing to marry me you would merely be adding another dimension to that agreement.'

Another dimension! Marriage! And to a man she already knew she was far too deeply and dangerously emotionally vulnerable to! Some dimension!

'But we are talking about marriage. And not…not a…a business contract,' Alice protested.

When he didn't reply, she turned away from him slightly, her voice muffled as she told him, 'For a man like you I expect that, historically in your family, marriage *is* usually a business arrangement, but in my family, for me…' She stopped and shook her head.

'I thought you loved Angelina,' Marco said softly.

Alice could feel herself weakening.

'I do,' she acknowledged, unable to resist looking at the baby as she did so, feeling her heart melt with love for her. Yes, it melted with love for Angelina, and it overheated with the adult form of exactly the same emotion for Marco, she reflected grimly, although he quite plainly did not feel the same way about her!

'I don't think you've given enough thought to what you're suggesting,' she told Marco valiantly, fighting hard to stave off her own potential downfall. 'You know very little about me. I might not have the right…qualifications to be Angelina's mother.'

She struggled for some logical way to make him see that what he was suggesting was impossible and then reminded him with relief, 'After all, I tried to steal your car.'

'No, you didn't,' Marco countered her admission coolly. 'The young lady who was with you was the thief, you simply took the blame to protect her.'

'You knew that!' Alice gaped at him, unable to conceal her astonishment.

'I knew it.' Marco confirmed.

'But you never said anything. You…'

'Do you really think I would have even entertained the thought of employing you to look after Angelina had I thought you had been the thief?' He shook his head, answering his own question as he told her, 'No way. The reason I was so determined to hire you was because I could see just how loyal and protective a person you were. And because I knew just how desperately Angelina needed someone like you. No, not someone *like* you. Only you,' he corrected himself softly. 'There is no one else like you, Alice, not for Angelina. Surely you can't desert her now, knowing how much she needs you. Knowing how attached to you she has already become? She has lost so much already in her short life. Her mother…her father…'

He was pulling all her emotional strings at once, and very powerfully so too, Alice acknowledged, but if she had any sense she would resist the pressure he was putting on her.

If she had any sense. Since when has anyone in love possessed that quality? she asked herself ruefully, and she was in love twice over…once with Angelina…and a second time with him!

'And as for you not having the right qualifications! You have the only qualification Angelina needs. Your love for her!'

'This is crazy,' she protested.

'No!' Marco corrected her. 'What would be crazy would be for Angelina to be handed over to Francine to have her life destroyed as she destroyed her poor, wretched daughter's life.'

Alice knew that he was speaking the truth. And as Marco had already stated, logically, there was really very little difference in working for him as Angelina's nanny for the next five years and remaining with her for the same period as his wife in name only.

How could she desert Angelina when she needed her in her life so much?

How could she agree to a business arrangement of a marriage with Marco when she loved and wanted him so much?

Hadn't this afternoon taught her anything at all?

'Yes!' That he was the most wonderful man to be kissed by, she found herself thinking recklessly.

Hastily she called her thoughts to order, reprimanding herself for her own foolishness.

There would be no more kisses between them, she reminded herself sternly. From now it was going to be strictly business between them!

Marco frowned as he heard the demanding knock on the door of his study. It was nearly midnight and he had been working for the last three hours, coming to his study immediately after dinner.

Tomorrow, before he firmly asked Francine to leave, he intended to make it clear to her that there was no way she could expect to take Angelina away from him.

Thinking of Angelina made him think of Alice, though, and thinking of Alice made him ache for the feel of her delicious body in his arms, and her equally delicious mouth against his own, just as it had been this afternoon.

'Marco, I know you're in there.'

His frown deepened as Francine walked in.

'I've been thinking...about Angelina,' she told him coolly. 'She is my granddaughter and that means the world to me, but I can see the situation from your point of view. Aldo was your closest relative and your heir and now that he is dead...' She gave a small shrug. 'I can make things easy for you, Marco, or I can make them difficult.'

He watched her, without saying anything, but then there was no need for him to do so; he had already guessed the real purpose of her visit to the *palazzo*!

'If you could, for instance, see your way to...putting a certain sum of money at my disposal, I am sure we can come to some mutually beneficial agreement over Angelina's future. I am thinking in terms of, say...' She paused and gave another small shrug.

'Well, let us say, for instance, one million dollars... That is hardly anything to you, Marco. You are a very, very wealthy man...'

'You want to sell me your granddaughter, is that what you are saying?' Marco asked her bluntly. 'I had heard that you had attempted to sell your daughter to the highest bidder—'

'How dare you say that?' she stopped him, her face an unpleasant shade of red.

'I dare say it because it is the truth. You put Patti into the meat market the minute she was old enough to be there.'

'She had a very wealthy boyfriend when she was modelling,' she interrupted him.

'A wealthy boyfriend...' Marco's mouth compressed angrily. 'The man was over three times her age and already married. You sold her to him.'

'She wanted to be with him.' She was almost screaming at him now. 'She enjoyed being with him a damn sight more than she enjoyed being with your tight-fisted cousin. When I think of the opportunities she lost because of him... She wanted to leave him. Did he tell you that? She was going to come to LA... He killed her.'

'No, if anyone killed both of them it was you, Francine. You were the one who destroyed their marriage with your greed, and your soulless craving for money. History repeats itself, doesn't it? You sold your daughter and now you want to sell her child to me. One million dollars, you say...'

Slowly Marco shook his head. He was tempted to give in and pay her, but he knew that if he did the matter wouldn't end there. Francine would come back wanting more money and then more.

Marco didn't trust Francine at all. He disliked her and he knew that she felt exactly the same way about him and that if she thought she could hurt or damage him in any way at all she would try to do so. Even if that meant damaging her own granddaughter.

She was starting to scream at him, telling him that she would make him pay for not acceding to her demands, that if he had really cared about Angelina, really wanted her, he would have been glad to pay her.

It was half an hour before she finally realised that he was not going to give in and left, hurling insults and threats at him as she did so.

Listening impassively to her, Marco made himself a silent promise that he would never, ever allow her to subject Angelina to the same kind of abuse she had subjected Patti to! Now if anything he felt it was even more imperative that he and Alice should marry.

CHAPTER EIGHT

ALICE had agreed to marry Marco! Marco was going to be her husband; she was going to be his wife. But in name only, Alice reminded herself quickly as she got shakily out of bed and went to see if Angelina had woken up.

The baby was still asleep, lying peacefully in her cot. Beyond the window of her room, the sky was a wonderful soft shade of blue, the morning sun shining on the gardens of the *palazzo*. Marco's home, her home for the next five years. But it would have been that anyway, Alice argued determinedly with herself. After all, her contract stipulated that she would work for Marco until Angelina was five.

Work for him, yes, but marry him!

She could always change her mind; walk away from him, and from Angelina! She could, but Alice knew that she wouldn't. It simply wasn't in her nature to abandon anyone who needed her, especially when that person was a helpless six-month-old baby.

And her own secret feelings for Marco? How was she going to cope with those for the next five years? How was she going to conceal them? They said that familiarity bred contempt—perhaps she would discover that playing the role of Marco's wife would banish those unwanted and dangerous feelings!

It was an argument that was so frail and full of potential minefields that Alice had no wish to pursue it.

She was going to marry Marco. Only to protect Angelina from Francine. Would Francine come to the nursery to see her granddaughter?

As she worked capably through her morning routine, Alice's head was full of anxious questions.

Angelina was awake now, and Alice, who had pulled a robe on when she had got up, picked her up and sat on the comfortable chair in front of the window, cuddling her and talking to her, enjoying the pleasure of their shared sleepy early-morning togetherness.

A couple of hours later when Alice's mobile started to ring, and she recognised that her sister was calling, she had no inner warning of what was to come as she answered the call.

'Alice?' her sister demanded excitedly, before Alice could even say hello. 'You dark horse, why on earth didn't you say anything? Not even a tiny hint! Mind you, Louise says that she isn't surprised and that it was obvious to her that the sparks were flying between you the first time you met.

'We couldn't believe it when Dad rang us first thing this morning to say that Marco had been on the phone to him to formally ask for your hand in marriage. Mum and Dad are both here now, by the way, and they want to talk to you. We're all really looking forward to coming over. Marco sounds wonderful, and we can't wait to meet him.

'It's really generous of him to want to fly us all out and put us up at the *palazzo*. It sounds so grand. Louise says that he is grand.'

Alice's head was reeling. Marco had telephoned her family and told them that they were going to be married—had formally asked for her hand in marriage—without a word of warning to her…without discussing what he planned to do with her?

Her sister was speaking to someone else, and Alice could hear her laughing.

'Louise is pretending not to be excited about being a bridesmaid, but of course she is. She says to tell you, though, that there's no way she is going to wear pink. Has Marco got a big family? I suppose he will have, being Italian… It's all so romantic… He obviously can't wait to marry you… Four weeks. It's no time at all. The parents want to have a word…'

Numbly Alice spoke to her parents, although after the call was over she couldn't honestly remember just what she had said to them or to her sister's husband, who had also wanted to congratulate her, and Louise, who had re-iterated her refusal to wear pink.

From her father she had learned that Marco had rung them first thing that morning to formally request her hand in marriage, and to invite her family over for the wedding, which he had informed him would take place in just under four weeks' time.

Picking up Angelina, Alice made her way downstairs. She needed to talk to Marco and right now!

In the main salon she bumped into Maddalena who beamed with pleasure when she saw her and came hurrying over to her.

'The *conte* has told us that you are to marry! You will make him a good wife and a loving mama for this little one,' she added as she stroked Angelina's face. 'Please God, in time there will be other little ones to keep her company.'

Other little ones! Alice digested her comment in silence, praying that the housekeeper wouldn't notice how hot her face had become! Of course it was only natural that she should assume that she and Marco would want to have children.

'I need to speak to Marco, Maddalena,' she told the housekeeper. 'Do you know where he is?'

'He is in the library,' Maddalena told her, giving her a roguish look that promptly made Alice's face burn even more hotly.

'And…er…Francine?' Alice asked hastily. She was surprised that the other woman had not been to the nursery to see Angelina.

Maddalena gave her a fulminating look and tossed her

head, saying contemptuously, 'That one. She has gone. She is no good. None of us like her.'

Her shocked disbelief drove out Alice's earlier self-conscious embarrassment. Francine had gone! Without making any attempt to see Angelina or to talk to her about her, to ask how she was, to check on her welfare, and to check Alice's suitability to have charge of her?

Alice tried to imagine anyone in her own family behaving in such a way and found that she couldn't.

Such behaviour appalled her and reinforced the dislike and distrust she had already felt towards Francine. So far as Alice was concerned Francine was totally unfit to have charge of a child. Her behaviour only confirmed Alice's belief that she had no real option other than to do whatever she could to protect Angelina.

Even if that meant marrying Marco?

Even if that meant marrying Marco, she told herself firmly.

She suspected that Marco had been right when he had told her that Francine's interest in Angelina had been totally mercenary, but it still hurt for the baby's sake to have her feelings so callously confirmed. No grandparent worthy of the name could surely have left without making at least some attempt to see her own flesh and blood?

She was halfway down the length of the huge formal salon, one of a series of interconnecting rooms of vast proportions and elegant architecture, when Marco suddenly appeared from the opposite direction.

'I was just on my way up to the nursery,' he said.

'I was looking for you.'

They both spoke together and then stopped, Marco's expression carefully watchful, whilst Alice was conscious that she was fumbling her words slightly and looking self-conscious.

'My sister has just telephoned me,' she told him when his silence told her that he was waiting for her to speak first. 'You had no right to speak to my family without telling me first,' she protested indignantly. 'They think now that...' She stopped and bit her lip.

'They think what?' Marco pressed her.

Angelina had fallen asleep against her shoulder and was a heavy weight in her arms, and, as though Marco sensed her discomfort, he commanded Alice, 'Give her to me. Are you all right now? Your heatstroke—?'

'I'm fine,' Alice assured him. 'Well, so far as my heatstroke goes. But I really wish you had spoken to me before telephoning my family. My parents. My sister. All of them now believe...they think...'

'They think what?' Marco encouraged her.

Alice could feel her face starting to burn a little with her own discomfort. He was the one who was responsible for the fact that her family thought their marriage was a love match, so why on earth should she be feeling self-conscious and guilty about explaining their misapprehension to him. And explain it she must, since he had taken the step of inviting them all to their 'wedding' because now they would assume...expect...

'They think that we...you... They think our marriage is going to be a...a normal one,' she managed to tell him, her face a soft pink with discomposure. 'Especially with you asking my father so formally, and...and inviting them all here for the wedding. Why did you do that?' she demanded accusingly.

'Because it was the right and proper thing to do,' Marco returned promptly. 'You are their daughter, I shall be their son-in-law.'

'But don't you see? Now they think.... They think that you and I...that we're in love,' Alice finally managed to burst out uncomfortably.

Marco shrugged dismissively. 'So...is that a problem?'

'Well, of course it is,' Alice told him forcefully. 'Now they will expect—' She stopped, her flush deepening as she unwantedly mentally visualised just what her family would be expecting when they arrived for the wedding. A loving couple who couldn't keep their eyes or their hands off one another. Who were eagerly exchanging whispers and kisses, who openly showed their love for one another. A couple, in short, deep in the throes of their new-found love.

'Our marriage is just a business arrangement and—'

'You were going to tell them that?' Marco challenged her in disbelief.

Alice grimaced. The truth was that she hadn't got as far as thinking just what she was going to tell her family, and in fact the craven thought had occurred to her that she really didn't need to tell them anything, since they already knew she would be asked to remain with Angelina until she reached school age.

'I wasn't going to say anything to them,' she was forced to admit when Marco continued to stand in front of her, automatically rocking Angelina in his arms as he waited for her reply.

'Not tell them anything!'

She could hear the reprimand and disbelief in his voice.

'I didn't want to complicate things,' Alice defended herself. 'After all our…our marriage is surely just a small extension of my contract… My family wouldn't have understood, they're old-fashioned and my sister…' Her voice trailed away unhappily.

'For this to work, for us to be able to convince a court that Angelina is in the right environment, it is essential that so far as everyone else is concerned this is a "normal" marriage,' Marco told her grimly. 'How do you think Francine would have reacted if she had found out that we were keeping our "marriage" a secret? That so far as your family were concerned you are merely working here? Do you really think she wouldn't have pounced on something like that with glee so that she could use it in court against us?'

There was nothing that Alice could say. She knew what he was saying made sense, and she knew too that it was impossible for her to explain to him how she really felt, not without running the risk of betraying her love for him!

'Whilst we are on the subject of our marriage,' Marco was continuing, 'That was why I was on my way to see you. I have made arrangements that the ceremony will take place at our local church four weeks from now. There will be other legal formalities to be gone through, as well as the religious ones, but these will not be too complicated. However, there will be a great deal to do here at the *palazzo*. I have already instructed Maddalena to take on the extra staff she will need. My family comprises several distant branches, filled, I am afraid to say, with some rather eccentric and elderly individuals who will all expect to be invited here to witness our marriage and share in its celebrations. Don't worry,' he told Alice when she made a small sound of shock. 'They will all fall on your neck with tears of gratitude, as they have been informing me that I should marry for many years now. However, my three eldest great-aunts all share a keen rivalry with one another, and one would need the skills of a Solomon to please them all.'

'Then why haven't you married?' Alice couldn't help asking him.

The frowning look he was giving her suddenly made her remember her first sighting of him. Now once more he was looking at her with that thoroughly arrogant disdain that made her own nerve endings prickle so sharply.

'Until now it hasn't been necessary,' Marco told her curtly.

'Necessary?' Alice shook her head in disbelief.

'People don't get married because it's "necessary",' she protested emotionally. 'They get married because they're in love. Because they can't bear not to be together.'

'So Aldo informed me,' Marco agreed dryly.

'Are you saying that love doesn't matter?' Alice challenged him, unable to prevent herself from asking the question. She didn't know why they were having this con-

versation, or rather she did, but she wished that she were
not being such a fool as to persist with it.

'Marriage for me has to be about more than mere sexual
desire,' Marco told her loftily. 'It has to be about a true
sharing of ideals and goals, of backgrounds and beliefs. It
has to be based on something that will last for a shared
lifetime and not burn out in a blaze of over-satiated lust.
In my opinion far too many people seek to sanitise physical lust by misnaming it love.'

His scornful dismissal of the importance of love warned
her of the fate she could expect if he were ever to recognise just how she felt about him. Before she could stop
herself, she was bursting out, 'I don't agree with you. I
think that love matters more than anything else, and…and
I always will. I would hate to be the kind of person who
thinks that it doesn't matter. But I suppose to someone like
you…'

'What do you mean someone like me?' Marco demanded. He didn't like her criticism and what he liked
even less was his own fierce reaction to it.

A little uncomfortable now about her outburst, Alice
tried to placate him.

'Well, it's obvious that a man like you—a man in your
position, with your family background,' she amended hastily when she saw the ominous way he was frowning at
her, 'would think of marriage in different terms to someone like me. I expect that you are used to the kind of
marriages where it's more about…about position and
wealth, than two people who love one another…' she finished. 'I suppose it's all about having different values.'

From the look in her eyes it was obvious to Marco that
she considered her own values to be vastly superior to his.

Infuriated, he was tempted to tell her that his parents'
marriage had been a fairy-tale love match, but instead he
chose another means of retaliation.

'Indeed it is,' he agreed smoothly. 'And as I have on

good authority, your values, unlike mine, are very modern.'

Alice's forehead crinkled into a small frown of incomprehension.

'What are you trying to say?' she demanded warily.

Marco gave her a savage look.

'As you have just pointed out, we are two different people from two different cultures, and, whilst I know how totally and completely committed you are to the children in your care, your moral values are not the same as mine.'

'My moral values?' Alice interrupted him sharply.

Marco looked away from her briefly before telling her, 'I know about your...affair with your previous boss.'

Alice was totally unable to make any response. What on earth was he talking about?

No way would she ever, ever even contemplate having an 'affair' with any married man, or any man loosely attached to someone else! The very thought revolted her.

'It was mentioned in the letter I received from his wife, in response to my request for a reference. She said that you were the best nanny she had ever had, but that her husband had confessed to having sex with you! She also hinted that there might have been other employer's husbands...who had enjoyed your...favours.'

Alice had always suspected that Pauline Levinsky had harboured an irrational resentment against her because she'd felt that Alice had been closer to her children than she'd been herself. But for her to do something like this!

Alice could vividly remember the day she had gone to Pauline and tactfully explained to her that instead of relocating to New York with the Levinsky family she had decided that the time had come for her to leave. It had been Pauline herself who had brought up the subject of her husband, Clive, and who had directly asked Alice if Clive was the reason she wanted to leave. And it was Pauline as well who had apologised when Alice had finally reluctantly admitted that she was leaving because she felt uncomfortable about Clive's increasingly possessive attitude towards her, coupled with his constant references to his sexual frustration.

She could remember how grateful she had felt towards Pauline when her boss had immediately offered her an apology.

How could Pauline have done this to her? Alice felt sickened, humiliated, too hurt to realise what Marco's real opinion of her was to even attempt to explain or to defend herself.

When she was finally able to speak all Alice could say was, 'You believe something like that about me but you want to marry me?'

Marco narrowed his eyes slightly as he heard the anger trembling in her voice. Her reaction wasn't what he had expected. He admired the fact that she had made no attempt to explain or deny anything, but the stark look in her eyes surprised him.

'Angelina is my prime concern here,' Marco replied coolly. 'My only concern,' he underlined pointedly. 'And so far as our marriage is concerned, it is merely a business arrangement,' he reminded her. 'Were I looking for a proper wife...' He paused, but Alice knew immediately what he was thinking.

'You would never choose me? Well, I would never want you either,' she lied fiercely. 'When I get married, properly married, I want it to be to someone I love so...so much that I can't bear to live without him. Someone who believes in love and who cherishes and values it,' she told him passionately.

What he had just said to her had hurt her very badly, and instinctively she wanted to defend and protect herself. His cynical misjudgement of her hadn't just hurt her, it had also put a totally different slant on the fact that he had kissed her. Did he think she was the kind of woman who slept around? With married men?

She knew that if it hadn't been for Angelina she would

have turned on her heel and walked out, torn up her contract and booked herself a seat on the first flight home.

But she simply could not do that to the little girl.

A new and totally untenable hideous thought struck her; a question bubbling to her lips that she had to ask.

'If you thought…if you believed…that about me, why did you employ me?' she demanded huskily.

Marco studied her.

As much to punish himself as punish her, he told her silkily, 'Well, it wasn't because I wanted to share the favours you've been giving to others.'

The fury of the look she shot him made him grimace ruefully. Were all women naturally good actors?

'Originally, you were the only applicant who fulfilled all of my criteria. Had I received Pauline Levinsky's letter before you had begun working for me and before Angelina had so obviously bonded with you, then no doubt I would not have employed you. However,' he continued coolly, 'so far as your, er…predilection for other women's husbands goes, it is not an issue, since I do not have a wife. Fortunately, by the time Angelina is old enough to need a moral role model…'

'I will be out of her life,' Alice completed bitterly for him. What on earth had she got herself into?

'Now,' Marco was continuing, as though the bombshell he had just dropped meant nothing, 'to get back to the matter in hand. You will of course need to make a visit to Milan to appoint a designer to make your wedding gown, and those of your attendants. I understand my friend the young car thief will be one of them, and also that she most assuredly will not wear pink.'

Alice stared at him. How could he indulge in humour after what he had just said? If she had needed any proof that he felt no personal emotion for her whatsoever, she had just received it, Alice acknowledged.

To her chagrin, knowing that actually hurt her more than

knowing that he thought she was the kind of person who indulged in casual sex!

'I'm sure I can find something simple and off the peg here in Florence,' she told him dully. 'As you said yourself, our marriage is just a business arrangement, after all, and not a proper marriage. We don't love one another.'

Alice was proud of the way she had managed to deny her feelings. She just hoped that she would be able to go on denying them!

'It is still a marriage, and both our families will have expectations of it. Beliefs, which I do not intend to damage.'

Mercifully, before he could say anything else Angelina woke up and started to whimper. 'Maddalena told me that Francine has left,' Alice managed to steady her voice enough to say as she took Angelina from Marco, carefully making sure that she didn't accidentally come into physical contact with him as she did so, cuddling her until she had calmed down before laying her down.

After what he had just said to her, he must never, ever guess how she felt about him. Could he really not see that she was simply not the sort of person to indulge in the kind of behaviour he had accused her of? Theirs was a business relationship, entered into solely to protect the child they both loved, and from now on her pride must make sure that he never had any reason to suspect she had ever dreamed of it being anything else.

'Yes, she has,' Marco agreed.

'Do you think she will still try to take Angelina away?' Alice asked him, giving a small shiver of apprehension as she did so.

'What I think is that if she does, the fact that you and I will be married should ensure that Angelina stays where she belongs, with people who love her,' Marco told her firmly.

'Now, we have a great deal to discuss. We shall of course be hosting together a pre-wedding dinner for both our families, and a post-wedding party. It is a tradition in my family that when the heir marries, a large feast is held for the estate workers—but I shall make all the arrangements for that. I have invited your family to fly over to join us one week before the wedding; that should allow time for our little Ferrari thief to try on her bridesmaid's gown. Of course your sister will be your principal attendant. Since my great-aunts are extremely traditional, not to say old-fashioned in their outlook, they will as a matter of course expect us to be sleeping in separate rooms, so there should be no embarrassment on that score, although, whilst we are discussing such a delicate subject, I suspect that we shall be expected to indulge in the occasional display of mutual affection.'

'No!' Alice's face had gone paper-white, fear and anxiety sharpening her voice.

'No,' she repeated. Shaking her head vehemently, 'I won't. You can't expect me to do anything like that.'

The intensity and immediacy of her rejection brought a dark glitter of anger to Marco's eyes.

'You're overdoing the pseudo-virginal hysterics,' he warned her grittily. 'After all,' he continued unforgivably in a voice as smooth as honey, 'it isn't as though you're being asked to do anything you haven't done before, many, many times, and of course with far more intimacy.'

It was too much for Alice to bear. Blindly she retaliated, telling him fiercely, 'That was different. I didn't have to pretend, then. I wanted him…them…' she corrected herself recklessly as she saw the look in his eyes.

She gave a small, high-pitched cry of fear and panic as she was unceremoniously dragged into Marco's arms, and imprisoned there whilst his mouth savaged hers.

Innocent as she was, even Alice knew that it was a mistake to challenge a man sexually, and even more of one to imply that he was sexually inferior to another. That was no doubt why Marco was kissing her so passionately now, forcing her lips to part as his tongue thrust deeply into her mouth causing her whole body to shudder in tormented recognition of the sexual symbolism of his intimate kiss.

This was the kind of kiss a man gave to a sexually experienced woman, she realised, the kind of kiss that immediately propelled them both into a shockingly sensual place.

She felt his hand touching her body, boldly taking possession of her breast, expertly caressing its peak into a tormented nub of frantic longing. Dizzily Alice knew that ultimately she was going to hate herself for the way she was feeling, but she simply did not have the experience to fight back against such a sustained and erotic attack. Helplessly she swayed towards Marco, wanting to be even closer to him, her hand reaching up towards his jaw in her need to prolong the intimacy of his kiss, but as soon as she touched him he stepped back from her, manacling her wrists with his hands as he kept her at a distance, demanding, 'Now tell me that you were acting.'

There was nothing Alice could say. No way she could hide her shame.

'We can't do this,' she whispered in anguish.

'We can't not do,' Marco corrected her harshly. 'It's too late to change your mind now.'

His own behaviour had shocked him. He was behaving like a jealous lover!

CHAPTER NINE

MISERABLY Alice ducked her head as she and Marco came out of the renaissance church where, like them, so many of Marco's ancestors had been married.

Only she knew just how badly affected she was by this mockery of what should have been one of the most special and meaningful days of her life.

In a deliberate act of self-loathing, she had chosen not the pure white dress she was fully entitled to wear, but instead one that was a rich, warm cream.

'I thought it would cause too much comment if I wore scarlet,' she told Marco flippantly just as they left the church.

To her relief her family had fully understood and supported her determination to pay for her own dress and those of her attendants, although Marco had not been very pleased when she had told him of this decision.

'What's wrong? Are you afraid that it might not be good enough? You should have thought about that before you asked me to marry you,' she had thrown angrily at him. 'I am not letting you pay for my wedding dress.'

'We made a business arrangement,' Marco had reminded her grimly. 'And as part of that arrangement, naturally I am prepared to pay for any clothes you will need to support your new role.'

'I don't care what you say. You are not buying my wedding dress,' Alice had retorted.

And that had only been one of the fierce arguments they had had in the lead-up to their wedding day.

Unfortunately one of the most serious ones had been

one she had lost—and it had been over her engagement
and wedding rings.

When Marco had produced the huge ring that he had
told her was traditionally worn by the di Vincenti brides,
she had blanched in horror at the thought of wearing something so patently irreplaceable, but Marco had been insistent.

'My family will expect to see you wearing it,' he had
told her. And he had been right; the first thing his great-
aunts had looked for when she had been formally presented to them had been the family ring.

Unexpectedly, Alice had rather taken to Marco's great-
aunts. They made her laugh with their quaint, old-
fashioned ways, but she could see beneath their bravado
that they were three elderly ladies who felt apprehensive
about the way the modern world was going. None of them
had any children and so Marco, although both he and they
would have immediately denied it, obviously had a very
special place in their hearts.

From all of them she had learned about his childhood,
and his teenage years; the courage with which he had taken
on his father's mantle, the differences between him and
Aldo, whom they had all denounced as a very spoiled and
selfish young man, and from them she had learned too just
how important it was to them as a family that Marco continued the family line with children, especially a son of his
own.

She already knew, of course, just how strong his sense
of duty was; far, far stronger than his own feelings!

As she'd listened to them her heart had grown heavier
and heavier. No doubt one day Marco would have sons,
but of course she would not be their mother!

As their wedding guests pressed close to them to offer
them their congratulations, Alice looked towards her sister,
who had happily taken charge of Angelina.

Like Louise, she was wearing a dress in soft, shifting
layers of differently shaded lilac silk organza.

It suited her and Alice could tell her that her brother-in-law, Louise's father, thought so too.

As Louise picked up the train of her dress she rolled her eyes at Alice and told her in her newly acquired grown-up manner, 'Don't say anything, but I'm sure Dad is trying to persuade poor Connie to have a baby. Honestly, you'd think he'd have more sense.' She shook her head derisively. But Alice could see that she was far from averse to the idea of a stepsibling, and her heart lifted a little.

As she smiled at her Louise gave her an uncertain look and whispered gruffly, 'Thanks for not saying anything to them, about...you know what...'

The previous evening at dinner, the celebration family dinner, Marco had presented Louise with a beautiful gold charm bracelet and hanging from it had been a perfect miniature Ferrari.

The words of their so recently spoken vows were ringing still in Alice's head as she sat beside Marco as his wife for the lengthy formal dinner being given to celebrate their marriage. Over five hundred guests had been invited, despite the reservations and doubts Alice had raised when Marco had discussed his plans with her.

'It is expected. It would cause gossip if we didn't, and I don't intend to give Francine any ammunition to fire at us,' was all he had said when she had tried to protest that it surely made sense to keep their marriage low-key, especially in view of their inevitable ending of it.

The meal was over and the final toasts had been drunk. Angelina was lying fast asleep in her stroller at Alice's side.

Somehow, foolishly, perhaps, she had not realised just how she was going to feel when they exchanged their wedding vows, how momentous the occasion would be, how solemn and awesome; how portentous and binding the words were going to sound, and how both her senses and her body were going to react to them.

But it was too late now to feel that she had committed a sin against the sanctity of marriage and the sanctity of her love. She was Marco's wife.

In name only, she reminded herself shakily. It was a business arrangement, that was all.

In the ballroom, beyond the salon where they had eaten, they could see through the folded-back open double doors that the band was starting to play.

Alice frowned as she recognised that those people seated closest to them were all turning to look at them.

The speeches were over, surely?

'Alice…' she heard Marco saying formally as he pushed back his chair and stood up.

What was he expecting her to do? Confused, she looked at her sister, who laughed and told her softly, 'Everyone's waiting for you and Marco to begin the dancing. It's tradition that the bride and groom have the first dance, remember.'

Of course… Flushing, Alice pushed back her own chair, conscious of how warm and strong Marco's hand felt as he took hold of her. She saw him frown as he felt the icy coldness of her fingers.

Her eyes felt heavy with the tears she knew she must not shed; tears for all that this day should have meant and all that would now be denied to her for ever. She knew that, no matter what her future held, this day would cast its shadow over any happiness she might have had for ever.

They were on the dance floor now, with Marco drawing her closer, so close that she could feel the beat of his heart against her own body, fierce, thunderous. Dangerous. She missed a step and trembled as he held her closer, instinctively looking up at him and then wishing that she hadn't.

She could see the firm thrust of his chin, the full, warm curve of his bottom lip. Her trembling became more intense and she could feel his hand tightening around hers. He smelled faintly of the cologne he wore and a taunting, sensual Marco smell that made her ache to close her eyes and just stand there breathing it in. Breathing him in, and impressing on her mind for ever this heartbeat of time.

The slow strains of the old-fashioned romantic waltz filled her ears, the heat of Marco's body enveloping her. She felt as though they were enclosed in a small, private island of their own, an island where nothing else existed, only the way she felt about him and the way she longed for him to feel about her.

She missed another step and gasped as he held her, almost lifting her against his body.

'You're tired.' He made it sound like an accusation.

'No,' she denied.

The intimacy of dancing with him like this on the day of their wedding, their marriage, brought an emotional lump to her throat. Abruptly the music stopped, bringing her back to a reality she didn't want. In his arms she had been able to imagine…to pretend… She made to turn away from him but he restrained her.

'Our guests are waiting,' he told her.

Puzzled, she asked him, 'What for?'

'For this,' he responded, drawing her back against his body and slowly wrapping one arm around her before cupping the side of her face with his free hand, tilting her face up towards his own.

His kiss was slow and measured, savouring her mouth, an intimate act for a public audience, made all the more shocking and dangerous somehow by the fact that outwardly he made it look so tender whilst inwardly she knew it meant nothing at all. At least not to him.

When he finally released her their guests were clapping and laughing. Fiercely Alice blinked away her threatening tears.

Other couples were joining them on the dance floor now. Alice pulled away from Marco.

'I want to go and check on Angelina.'

'Your sister is with her,' he reminded her.

'She is my responsibility,' Alice insisted stubbornly. 'She is why you have married me, after all.'

'And why you have married me,' Marco responded.

'You must be disappointed that you aren't having a honeymoon.'

Alice shook her head as she listened to her sister. It was two o'clock in the morning and the festivities were finally over.

'No, I'm not,' she told her, truthfully.

They had reached the top of the stairs, and Alice turned automatically to head for the nursery.

Laughing, Connie stopped her. 'Where are you going?' she asked her. 'The master bedroom suite is that way...'

'Oh... Yes. But Angelina...'

'Maddalena and I have moved Angelina's things into the master suite for you,' Connie told her with a gentle smile. 'Marco explained that there hadn't been an opportunity yet for the two of you to redecorate the rooms he had been using, and that you planned to do that together. I don't suppose Angelina will mind sleeping in his dressing room for the time being, though. Not when she's got the two of you so close to her...'

Alice swallowed nervously as she listened to her sister. Foolishly perhaps, she had not really given any thought to where she would be sleeping once she and Marco were married. Somehow she had assumed that she would simply go on sleeping in her room in the nursery suite, but it seemed that she had been wrong.

As she hesitated outside Marco's bedroom door, it suddenly opened and Marco himself was standing there.

'One bride,' her sister told him mischievously before adding, 'Is Angelina okay? Maddalena and I checked on her an hour ago.'

'She's fine. Fast asleep,' Marco responded, standing back from the doorway, and somehow without knowing quite how it had happened Alice discovered that she had walked inside and that the door was being closed, shutting her in the room with Marco.

She had not been in his bedroom before, and she glanced round it quickly and nervously. Like all the rooms in the *palazzo* it was huge, and furnished in what she guessed were priceless antiques.

'I can't sleep in here,' she told him huskily, panic suddenly filling her.

'I'm afraid you not only can, but must!' Marco informed her coolly. 'After all, it's what everyone will expect. We are now man and wife.'

'Yes, but only because of Angelina…I… You said this was going to be a marriage in name only.'

'Which it is, but you can't sleep apart from me tonight, of all nights. Surely you must realise that?' Marco told her giving her, a grim look as he added derisively, 'You're off stage now, Alice. You can forget the wide-eyed virgin-bride look! And you can forget anything else as well. I shall spend the night in my dressing room. There is a bed in there. After our guests have left tomorrow we will have time to talk about the future properly.'

Alice felt too unhappy to argue with him or to protest at his high-handedness.

And besides, if she did she suspected he would only deride her.

'The bathroom is through there,' Marco told her, indicating one of the two doors opening off the bedroom.

'Your sister and Maddalena have brought some of your things from your own room, I believe…' he added before going into the dressing room and closing the door behind him.

Some of her things… Which of them? Alice wondered worriedly.

It was her habit to sleep in nothing other than her own skin, a sensual pleasure she especially enjoyed indulging in at the *palazzo* where the bed linen was cool, crisp cotton, smelling of fresh air and herbs. However, the thought of padding naked around a room with Marco in such close proximity was not one she felt in any way relaxed about.

Had her sister thought to bring her a robe, or had she assumed that, as a new bride, Alice would neither want nor need to wear any such thing?

Marco stared broodingly out of the dressing-room window into the soft darkness of the night, trying to come to terms with his feelings, and the simple truth he had had to confront.

From the moment Alice had come into his life she had unwittingly challenged his own beliefs, overturning things about himself he had thought were set in stone. He had tried to resist, telling himself that it was for Angelina's sake that he had been able to recognise how much she was able to give the baby in terms of love, and how much more important that was than the differences that existed between their sexual moral codes.

He had tried to dismiss his own desire for her as an unimportant irritation that could be ignored; he had even, shamefully, at one point, tried to find some way of convincing himself that Alice had deliberately incited it, but thankfully his conscience had refused to co-operate.

Instead he had tried to separate Alice into two different people: the Alice whose love for Angelina was unconditional and unquestionable, and whom he just had to watch with the baby and he was filled with the fiercest and purest emotions it was possible for him to feel, and the Alice who'd thought nothing of having sex with a married man.

Over the past few weeks, the Alice who gave herself so unstintingly to Angelina's care had touched his emotions more and more deeply. And as for the Alice who had apparently given herself equally unstintingly to her lovers—Marco closed his eyes, a muscle tensing in his jaw.

There was no point in lying to himself any longer—the emotion motivating him when he thought of that Alice was not self-righteous disapproval, but raw, male jealousy.

He might genuinely have been prompted to suggest a marriage between Alice and himself as a means of protecting Angelina, but today, standing in church beside her, he had known that he was marrying her because he loved her.

And the Alice he loved was the whole Alice; all of her; just as she was perfect. He had no right to judge her. It was his jealousy and his perhaps outdated beliefs that were at fault, and not Alice herself.

Earlier in the evening dancing with her, holding her in his arms, breathing in her perfume, he had ached so badly for her, but there was no way now that sex alone could ever be enough to appease his hunger for her.

Outside in the main bedroom Alice suddenly frowned. She had removed her veil and her headdress earlier in the evening but she was still wearing her wedding dress, and she now realised that unless she asked for Marco's help in removing it she was going to have to spend the night sleeping in it, since it fastened all the way down the back with a long row of tiny little buttons.

No doubt it would cause a stir if she appeared at breakfast in the morning still wearing her wedding gown!

Walking a little unsteadily to the closed dressing-room door, she knocked self-consciously on it, and called out hesitantly, 'Marco.'

Pausing in the act of unfastening his shirt buttons, Marco went to open the door.

Alice felt her heart starting to thud far too heavily as she looked at him, one hand lazily unfastening the buttons on his shirt whilst he stood there, his mouth slightly twisted in an expression she couldn't understand.

'I'm sorry to disturb you,' she began and then stopped. Did her voice sound as betrayingly nervous and self-conscious to Marco as it did to her?

She touched the side of her throat, her fingers playing

with her hair, and then tensed. There was something about the way Marco was watching her.

Had his expression changed, or was it simply the shadows that were giving him that hooded, dangerous look that was making her heart beat so fiercely fast?

Desperate to evade his gaze, Alice dragged her own away only to discover that it was now resting where his unfastened shirt was revealing a dark expanse of hard-muscled torso, finely covered in soft dark hair.

Marco was her husband; she was his wife; they had just been married.

A fine shudder of reaction skittered over her body as her emotions overwhelmed her. The intensity of her own longing, her own love made her feel dizzy. Alice swallowed. Hard. Very hard…and not because she felt nervous. No way did she feel nervous. No, what she felt was…

Her arm had actually lifted of its own volition, her fingertips aching to delve into that sexy, silky darkness, and explore that soft, silky evidence of his maleness, before she somehow managed to stop herself.

Her throat had gone dry, her tiredness forgotten. Desperately she tried to remind herself of just why she had gone to him.

'I…I need some help with my dress,' she managed to whisper. 'The buttons…' To show him what she meant she turned round.

'I can't unfasten them,' she explained.

'Yes, I can see what you mean.'

She had never heard Marco's voice sound so terse.

'I can't sleep in my dress.' Why wasn't he doing anything? She could feel the searing heat of his breath against the exposed nape of her neck. It made her ache to be closer to him, to turn round and demand, beg that he treat her as a woman and not as a business partner.

'I can't ask anyone else.' Her voice trembled and her face burned with the humiliation of knowing just how dan-

gerously close she was to making a complete fool of herself.

Marco did not share her feelings; she already knew that.

'No,' she heard him agreeing, his voice deep and un-
familiarly strained. 'You can't.'

'Your dress makes your waist look tiny,' Marco told her,
unexpectedly spanning it with his hands. His voice
sounded different somehow, deeper, thicker, and Alice
knew that there was a betraying tremble in her own as she
responded automatically.

'It's the boning inside it.'

'Boning?' Marco sounded bemused. 'I thought that went
out with the Victorians,' he commented as he began to
carefully unfasten the tiny buttons.

Tensing her body against any betraying reaction to him,
Alice gritted her teeth.

There was a tallboy with a mirror on it in front of her
and in it she could see her own reflection and Marco's as
he slid the tiny loops over the even smaller buttons, but it
wasn't the sight of his dark hands busily unfastening her
dress that suddenly caused her to draw in her breath. No,
it was the realisation that once the dress was completely
unfastened and unsupported it would slither from her
shoulders, and all she was wearing underneath it was a
tiny pair of briefs. No bra, no hose, just a minute pair of
silk briefs.

Marco had reached the small of her back. Alice could
feel the heavy weight of her dress starting to drag it down-
wards, another few buttons and it would… She started to
panic, trying to pull away from him.

'Wait,' he instructed her, refusing to let go. 'I haven't
unfastened them all yet.'

Not all of them maybe, but he had unfastened enough
of them, Alice recognised as her dress slid to the floor with
a whoosh before she could grab hold of it.

Frozen with self-consciousness, Alice couldn't move.

In the mirror her gaze met Marco's, her colour getting

higher with every breath she took. Marco looked as though he had been turned to stone, as immobile as she was herself apart from the fierce glitter darkening his eyes. She heard him breathe a harsh, ragged sound that brought her skin out in a rush of sensual goose-bumps, and galvanised her into protective action.

As though they had actually felt the heat of that breath on them, her nipples pouted and stiffened. Instinctively Alice tried to conceal what was happening to her from him; the urge to lift her hands and cover her breasts was automatic.

But shockingly Marco reacted faster, so that it was his hands that covered her nakedness, cupping their soft shape, concealing their flaunting arousal.

'Alice! Alice!' she heard him groan in a tone of voice she had never heard him use before, deep raw, hungry, making her shiver with excitement and longing.

He bent his head and kissed the side of her throat, causing a million zillion quivers of wild, frantic delight to soar through her.

'Have you any idea what you're doing to me?' he demanded thickly. 'Do you know how tempting this is? You are?' he whispered roughly. 'Far, far too tempting!' he answered his own question, his voice thick with desire. 'Do you know what you're doing to me? How much you are making me want you?'

Alice certainly knew what he was doing to her, and how very, very tempted, how shockingly, achingly tormented she was!

He was turning her round, so that her naked breasts were pressed tightly against his equally naked chest, his hands sliding down her back to pull her right into his body, and then cupping the soft, rounded shape of her buttocks.

She could feel how aroused he was. Knowing that he wanted her made her feel sensually powerful, increasing her longing for him.

Ruthlessly she ignored the tiny voice trying to remind

her that he did not love her, and that his sexual arousal was just an automatic male reaction to her nakedness.

She didn't want the truth.

No, what she wanted was the fantasy of believing that he loved her.

Without knowing she had done so, she breathed his name, exhaling it in a soft, enticing sound of intimate invitation and desire.

It ran over Marco's senses like a small electric current, heightening everything he was already feeling. It was impossible for him to resist her.

He could feel her body quivering beneath his touch; reality was being consumed in the fiercely burning fires of his desire.

He kissed her forehead and then her eyelids, her cheek and the shockingly responsive place just behind her ear, making Alice moan openly in aching pleasure.

Marco could feel his self-control slipping away. He kissed her mouth, slowly, carefully, trying to restrain himself. Her lips trembled beneath his and her hand gripped his shoulder, her fingers digging into his flesh as she shuddered against him.

She was irresistibly responsive, making him feel that she was powerless to control her reaction to him. It was a dangerously powerful aphrodisiac. For a second he hesitated, reminding himself that he was a man of honour and that their marriage was solely a business arrangement, at least so far as she was concerned, no matter how he might feel about her, but the feel of her against him was too much for his self-control.

'You want me?' he asked her, determined to let the decision be hers.

Alice tensed. Here was her chance to stop what was happening if she wanted to. She was poised on the brink of taking a step that once taken would change her life for ever. But hadn't her love for Marco already done that?

Wouldn't she regret it for the rest her life if she refused what he was offering her now?

Taking a deep breath, she nodded, and then just in case he hadn't understood she told him huskily, 'Yes, I want you.'

Such simple words, to make his heart ache with such heaviness and his body pulse with such longing, Marco acknowledged.

Cupping her face, he kissed her slowly, savouring every centimetre of her mouth with an intimacy that momentarily caught Alice off guard. His hands were caressing her body. Against her mouth he whispered, 'Aren't you going to undress me?'

Her undress him? Alice began to panic. She had forgotten that Marco believed her to be sexually experienced, and a seducer of married men!

Alice's stiffness and lack of response made Marco frown. Had she changed her mind?

He tried to look into her eyes, but she immediately dropped her lashes, veiling them from him.

'I think it might save time if you did that yourself.'

Alice didn't know how she had managed to find the courage to whisper the soft words. She felt as though her whole body were on fire with self-consciousness.

Save time! Marco was too engrossed in his own thoughts and feelings to register her discomfort. Picking her up, he carried her over to the bed, slowly lowering her onto it and leaning over her so that her breasts were pressed against the warm nakedness of his chest.

'You're right,' he told her thickly. 'We don't need to waste time on unnecessary preliminaries when what we both want is this!'

He was kissing her now in a way that shocked her nearly as much as it excited her. His hands shaped her naked breasts. As he ran the tip of his tongue round her softly swollen mouth he ran the pad of his thumb around her aching nipple.

Her whole body arched as though a bow had been drawn taut from her breasts to her sex. Unable to stop herself, Alice made a small pleading gasp of sound, which she tried to smother against Marco's shoulder, but instead of releasing her from her torment her reaction only caused him to increase it.

The way he was touching her nipples made her whole body shudder with desire. And the only way she could stifle the sounds of agonised need she was making was to bite sharply into the firm flesh against her lips, whilst her fingers clenched into the sheet, which the passionate thrashing of her body had ruckled.

The sensuality of her response to him was driving Marco out of his mind. Tugging at his clothes, he tore them off as quickly as he could without releasing her, knowing that he was simply not able to release her. The feel and taste of her, the scent and heat of her were like an immediately addictive drug.

The hand he had had to lift from her body to unfasten his trousers had left her breast exposed, its peak taut, tempting him, taunting him to respond to its erotic invitation. Dragging off the last of his clothes, he covered it with his lips, laving it fiercely with his tongue before drawing it deeply into his mouth and sweetly savaging it with the raw sensuality of his need.

His hand slid down her body, parting her legs, seeking her warm, female heat.

Deep shudders ripped through Alice's body. She had thought she knew all about sex, and that experiencing it would hold no surprises for her, but the raw sexuality of what was happening was showing her how wrong she had been.

Somehow, without knowing how, she had buried her fingers in Marco's hair, holding his head against her breast as she submitted to the ferocity of the sensation that swept her in wave after wave.

She could feel the wet heat of her sex, and feel, too, the

way it was responding to Marco's touch, expanding, opening. His fingertip stroked and searched and then circled, and the nub of flesh normally so innocently dormant swelled and pulsed with pleasure.

'Marco. Marco.'

Barely aware that she was even speaking, never mind what she was actually inciting, Alice kept on repeating Marco's name in a frenzied litany of uncontrollable need.

Marco hesitated. He could sense how close she was to her fulfilment, but this first time for them together he wanted that fulfilment to be part of his.

Still stroking her, he moved over her, kissing her passionately as he started to thrust into her.

Beneath his kiss Alice gasped, her eyes widening as she felt her body stretch to accommodate him. Oh, but it felt so good. He felt so good.

Helplessly she clung to Marco, overwhelmed by what she was feeling. All she knew was that the sharp pang of pain she was suddenly experiencing was somehow a part of the so much greater pleasure; that the feeling of being totally filled by him was one that she was enjoying too much to care about the pain.

Marco felt her body's tension, its tightness, he heard Alice's small cry but it was too late for him to stop what was happening. To withdraw now would be to risk hurting her even more. He tried to control his body's demand for completion, but it was too late.

Alice's fingers tightened into the hard muscle of Marco's arm as beyond the pain she could feel something else, somewhere else, a place so powerful and achingly sweet that tears filled her eyes at the thought of not reaching it. Desperately she pressed closer to Marco, silently willing him to take her there, and then miraculously that was what he did and the small, tiny waves of sensation moving with such wonderful pleasure inside her had become larger ones, thudding, rolling, curling, ocean-wide breakers of such pleasure that she could hardly bear to endure it.

In its aftermath her whole body felt as though it were humming with happiness. Drowsily she looked at Marco, trying to suppress her small, instinctive wince as he withdrew from her. She felt so tired. She could hardly keep her eyes open. She started to yawn.

Grimly Marco watched her.

CHAPTER TEN

'ALICE.'

Reluctantly Alice opened her eyes. Daylight was pouring in through the bedroom window and as Marco leaned over her, a towel draped round his hips, his body gleaming from the shower he had obviously just taken, she could see the scratch marks on his skin. Scratch marks she had inflicted last night at the height of her passion!

Miserably Alice tried to swallow. If she had been foolish enough to entertain some secret hope that last night's intimacy would somehow magically cause Marco to announce that he loved her, she knew now just how wrong she had been.

No words of love had passed his lips last night and, from the look she could see in his eyes, he certainly wasn't about to utter any now.

'Why didn't you tell me you were a virgin?' Marco asked her tersely.

He had been awake half the night mentally lashing himself for what he had done, for his crassness, his selfishness, his sheer male brutality in hurting her, but instead of telling her what he was actually feeling Marco heard himself sounding as angry as though she were the one at fault.

Marco's anger banished Alice's self-pity. Grabbing the sheet, she sat up in the bed and faced him. 'What was the point?' she challenged him. 'You had already decided that I was sexually experienced; a woman who seduced married men.'

She held her breath, waiting to see how Marco would react, willing him to tell her that he had never for a moment really doubted her. And then once he had done that

137

she wanted him to take her in his arms and tell her how much last night had meant to him and how it had made him realise that he loved her.

But of course he did no such thing. Instead he walked towards the window and stood there with his back to her.

'You do realise that this changes everything between us, don't you?' he told her.

She could hear from his voice just how seriously he was taking things.

'How could my virginity do that?' she asked him uncertainly.

She could hear his irritated indrawn breath.

'How could it not? Do you think I am the kind of man who goes around deflowering virgins?' He stopped and shook his head, swinging round to focus on her. 'Do you imagine that I like knowing that my…my desire was so out of control that I could not restrain myself? We will talk later about Mrs Levinsky's reasons for lying to me about you, but I think I guess what they were. Jealousy is a very dangerous weapon. I have no excuses to offer you for what…what happened. You are now my wife in every sense of the word. It is my duty, my responsibility…'

'No,' Alice protested, struggling to come to terms with what he was saying. 'We made a business arrangement, that is all.'

'Last night changed all that irrevocably,' Marco told her implacably. 'Do you realise that you could be carrying our child…my child?' he threw at her.

Alice gripped the sheet ever harder. A baby. Marco's baby… She could feel herself melting, yearning…and she had to fight to hold onto reality.

'We must both hope that you are not,' Marco said sternly.

He didn't want her to have his child?

'We have agreed that our marriage will end in five years' time,' Marco reminded her as though he sensed what she was thinking. 'I considered myself to be honour bound to stand by that arrangement. However, if you were to have my child, there is no way I could allow him or her to be brought up by anyone other than myself.' He paused and looked past her before continuing, 'And knowing what I do about you I know that you will feel the same way. You have very strong feelings about love. I know that. I cannot compound what I have already done by tying you to a loveless marriage.'

Alice's heart had started to thump far too heavily. There! He had told her now that he did not love her. How much more plainly did she need to hear it?

As though her silence exasperated him, he grated harshly, 'Why did you let it happen, Alice? To punish me for misjudging you? To make an irrevocable, unassailable point? Didn't you think…?'

No matter why she had done it, he was the one who was at fault. Marco knew that. But he also knew that the reality of starkly putting into words that she did not love him was tearing him apart.

This wasn't a pain he was going to have to endure for a matter of weeks or months, but for the rest of his life!

Dangerously close to tears, Alice glared at him.

'Didn't you think?' she challenged him.

'Think? In the state I was in?' Marco's expression was self-derisory.

He could see Alice starting to frown and he cursed himself inwardly. If he wasn't careful he was going to reveal to her how he felt about her, and that was a burden he was fiercely determined he was not going to place on her.

At least he hadn't guessed how she felt about him, Alice comforted herself. At least she was to be spared that humiliation.

'It seemed a good idea at the time,' she responded, giving a small toss of her head.

'A good idea?'

She could see the way Marco's throat constricted as the

words were ripped from it. He was looking at her as though he would like to strangle her.

'How could you behave so irresponsibly, throw yourself away so casually…? Especially when…'

He stopped, but Alice guessed what he had been about to say. Especially when he didn't love her and she meant nothing whatsoever to him.

Marco tried to calm himself down. He knew the demands pride and self-respect could make on a person, but for Alice to go to such dangerous lengths. Had she no sense of self-preservation?

'It wasn't really that important,' Alice told him with a bravado she was far from feeling. The truth was that it was only the most important thing she had ever done! 'At my age virginity can get to be something of an embarrassment, and, besides, I thought it was time I found out what all the fuss is about!'

She felt she ought to get that in, just to make sure she had made it plain to him that she was not foolish enough to be dreaming dreams of love.

Marco could scarcely believe his ears. He watched her through narrowed eyes. She sounded convincing enough, but something, some instinct, told him that she was lying to him. Why? Was she aware of the challenge she was issuing? And the way his own instincts were leaping to meet it, and to show her right here and now just how much pleasure her body was capable of?

Grimly he decided to teach her a small warning lesson, for her own sake as well as his!

'Indeed,' he responded silkily. 'Dare I hope that I came up to your expectations?'

Uneasily Alice rubbed her tongue-tip round her nervously dry lips. She knew she had been deliberately goading him.

Unable to risk looking directly at him, she told him as insouciantly as she could, 'It was… It was interesting, but not something I would want to repeat.'

Marco stared at her. He was tempted to let himself believe that she was deliberately trying to incite him. If he thought for one minute that she actually wanted... But then she turned her head and he saw the dark bruise on her collar-bone—a bruise he himself must have inflicted at the height of his passion—and guilt poured through him, filling him with self-contempt.

It was bad enough that he had taken her virginity. He wasn't going to let himself be so weakened by his love for her that he used it as an excuse to keep her in his bed. In five years' time he wanted to be able to keep his promise to her to set her free. It was a matter of honour to do so, but if she should conceive his child Marco knew there was no way he would ever be able to let either of them go.

'What happened between us last night must never happen again, Alice, and I intend to make sure that it does not!'

Alice could feel her face starting to burn at the humiliation of the warning he was giving her. Did he really think that she was so lacking in self-respect that she would try to initiate sex between them?

'Good. I'm glad to hear it,' she replied in a high, brittle voice.

For a second Marco had a dangerous impulse to take hold of her and make her retract her words. To caress her, kiss her, love her until she was crying out to him. For him. For his love!

He felt as though he were sinking in quicksand; as fast as he tried to control his feelings, they pulled him back down!

She was so innocent; so inexperienced that she had no idea just how special and rare what they had shared had been. The pleasure she had given him! The way her body had responded to him...welcomed him...clung to him...

Marco could feel the savage burn of his own renewed aching need.

He had to get away from her before he did something he would regret!

CHAPTER ELEVEN

GENTLY Alice removed the sample of fabric Angelina had picked up from her baby fingers.

Alice was trying to make a final choice for the new wallpaper and fabrics to decorate the new master bedroom suite.

The suite comprised two bedrooms, one of which was ostensibly going to be Angelina's room complete with a bed for 'emergencies' and a playroom off it, with another large room which supposedly would be Alice and Marco's.

In the meantime all three of them were still sharing Marco's existing suite, although Alice had managed to insist that Marco slept in his own bed whilst she slept in the smaller bed in the dressing room so that she could be closer to Angelina.

True to his word Marco had kept her at a distance, physically as well as emotionally. And that of course was exactly what she wanted! At least it was what her pride demanded she wanted! When he spoke to her his voice was terse, his desire to spend as little time with her as possible hurtfully obvious.

The new suite was also going to include two dressing rooms, a shower room, and a separate bathroom, as well as a small private sitting room, and it was Alice's responsibility to choose the décor for the entire suite, whilst Marco was naturally taking charge of all the architectural, design and building work.

Marco had been anxious to get the plans finalised because he was due to fly to Rome the following day for a series of business meetings about a major project he was involved in.

Tickling Angelina, who had now cleverly produced another new tooth, Alice glanced at her watch. It was virtually time for her to get changed for dinner—a formality that had bemused her a little at first, but that she had now grown accustomed to. And at least she had found a use for all those expensive little outfits of Angelina's!

Whilst she might have refused to allow Marco to provide her with a new wardrobe full of expensive designer clothes, there was no reason why Angelina shouldn't wear hers. As was customary with Italian families, Angelina, whilst too young as yet to join them at the table, was there with them whilst they ate their dinner, much to Alice's relief. At least with Angelina there she had someone to talk to, someone with whom she could behave naturally.

Somehow or other without ever discussing the subject she and Marco had evolved a system that allowed them both the privacy to use the bedroom and the bathroom without the other being present whilst at the same time maintaining the fiction of their newly married status.

Alice knew that logically speaking she ought to be grateful to Marco for his discretion and for the fact that he was adhering to the agreement they had made, but instead what she was actually feeling was a sense of rejection and loss; a feeling of being cheated of something that she as a woman should have been experiencing.

The truth was that her body ached far more now from the lack of Marco's possession than it ever had done before he had possessed it, humiliating though it was for her to have to admit as much.

Maddalena was a stickler for punctuality, and in exactly ten minutes' time dinner would be served in the small, at least by the *palazzo*'s standards, pretty dining room, which had originally been decorated by Marco's mother.

When Alice pushed the stroller into the room a few minutes later, she found that Marco was already there, standing with his back to her, and looking out of the

French windows that opened out onto a small, private, enclosed garden.

He had obviously opened the French windows because Alice could hear the sound of water splashing from the ornate stone fountain, which dominated the elegant courtyard.

Although he turned round when he heard them coming into the dining room, he didn't smile. He looked preoccupied and distant Alice recognised, a feeling that was intensified for her during the course of their meal, when he seemed to have retreated behind an invisible wall into a dark, brooding silence that she felt reluctant to break.

After they had finished eating and Alice made to take Angelina upstairs to put her to bed, Marco announced abruptly that he intended to go with them.

'I shall be leaving early tomorrow morning for Rome,' he told Alice tersely. 'You've got my mobile number—please don't hesitate to use it if you need to reach me for any reason.'

Nodding, Alice suspected that he was thinking back to Angelina's illness. Happily the little girl had gone from strength to strength since then, and was now rosily chubby, and eating well enough even to please Alice's exacting standards.

'Angelina is going to miss you,' she told him as he helped her upstairs with the stroller. 'She could really do with a high chair now,' she commented once they had reached the bedroom.

'She can't feed herself yet, of course, but the sooner she gets used to eating with us, the better... I was wondering if it would be all right for me to go into Florence and buy one whilst you're away...'

'What...? Oh, yes. Of course. Get whatever you need, Alice.'

Alice frowned as she heard the tension in his voice. Something was wrong. She could sense it. By the time she re-emerged into the main bedroom half an hour later, to

confirm to Marco that she had finally made up her mind
about which fabric she wanted for their bedroom curtains,
Alice was feeling anxiously on edge. But abruptly her own
anxiety evaporated as she saw that Marco, obviously unaware of her presence, was standing beside the tallboy,
frowning down at the photograph of his cousin Aldo that
he was holding.

Alice felt her heart contract in a bittersweet pain of sad-
ness and compassion as she looked at him.

Only two photographs had decorated the tallboy on their
marriage. One had been of Marco's parents together with
him as a little boy and the other had been of his cousin.

Now there were three photographs there, the new ad-
dition being one of herself on their wedding day with
Angelina.

She had been shocked at first to see it there, but then
she had reasoned that it was perhaps there because Marco
felt that the other members of his household would expect
it to be there.

'Marco.'

She said his name quietly, and was not surprised when
he did not immediately respond to her.

Slowly he replaced the photograph and then turned
round.

'Today would have been his birthday,' he told her sombrely. 'He would have been twenty-seven…'

'For as long as I live I will never, ever forget the scene
I witnessed when I was called to the accident,' he added
grimly. 'Nor will I ever stop feeling that there was something I could have done to prevent it. Something I should
have done.'

'No. You mustn't say that,' Alice protested immediately, forgetting her own feelings, as she was swamped by
concern and compassion for him. Going over to him, she
touched his arm as tenderly as she would have done had
he been Angelina.

'He was an adult, Marco. A man. He made his own decisions...'

'Did he?' Marco asked her grimly. 'Or did Patti and I make them for him? It's true that I never wanted them to marry...but God knows I never wanted this.'

The feel of his flesh beneath her fingertips was distracting her, making her think. Making her want him. Hastily Alice moved back from him, unaware of the look he was giving her as she did so.

He stopped speaking and looked away from her. 'I used to chide him for his lifestyle, for living so...so...' He shook his head. 'But at least I can comfort myself—if indeed it is a comfort—that he enjoyed life to the full. That he lived it to the full. That he experienced love, shared it, even if it was in my eyes a shallow-rooted, ephemeral emotion and not what I myself would want. He conceived a child...the only way humans have of defying our mortality.'

Wisely Alice made no attempt to speak. She could sense that he needed to unburden himself, to vocalise his own feelings of bitterness and loss.

As he moved towards the desk in front of the bedroom window, Alice was surprised to see an open bottle of wine on it. Although Marco drank wine with his meals—as indeed she was now learning to do so herself—she had never before seen him touch alcohol at any other time, and yet here he was now filling his glass with the rich ruby liquid and lifting it to his lips, drinking deeply.

'He was the youngest member of my family, a brother to me almost. I never thought...'

He took another deep gulp of his wine. 'I felt protective towards him in the same way you do towards your charges, Alice, and the fact that he is dead makes me feel that I failed him. That there should have been some way I could sense what might happen, that I could have, should have done something to prevent it.'

And he took another deep swallow, virtually emptying his glass.

'How could you possibly have known?' Alice said gently, aching to comfort him.

'He only came here to the *palazzo* because he wanted me to hear his side of things, because he was concerned I would hear the gossip about the disintegration of his marriage from someone else. It was at my insistence that he brought Patti with him. I thought some time here together away from the distractions of Rome might help. But all it did was focus on the differences between them.

'When they left for the evening to go to Florence, I never dreamed that that would be the last time I would see them alive…'

He picked up the wine bottle, obviously intent on re-filling his glass, but instinctively Alice moved towards him, giving a small murmur of protest.

'No? No, you do not approve of me losing myself in drink…drowning out my pain in its embrace… But what alternative do I have?' Marco demanded harshly. 'You? My wife?' The bitterness of the brooding look he gave her shocked her. 'Would it disgust you to know that right now I ache so much that I could take you even without love?'

His words made Alice recoil with pain, but before she could say anything he was moving towards her, challenging her.

'I know already that you are woman enough to give your love to a needy child, but are you woman enough to let me lose myself in you, Alice? To drown out my pain in you; within you… To let me feel that I am alive, human…a man!'

She knew that it was the wine he had drunk and his pain that were making him say such things. And sex was a male anodyne, she knew that too!

Recklessly she made no attempt to move away from him, even though the voice of common sense within her was warning her that she should do so, and that if she stayed where she was Marco might quite legitimately take her presence as a tacit invitation.

That he might do exactly what he was doing, she recognised dizzily as he came towards her, and took hold of her, running his hands up and down her bare arms, his wine-scented breath dangerously seductive against her skin as he kissed her forehead and then the side of her throat.

'Let me… Let me lose myself in you, sweet Alice.'

The words of denial were on the tip of Alice's tongue. After all, she knew full well she ought to utter them, to put an end to this dangerous folly right now for both their sakes, but somehow they refused to be spoken as her body responded to Marco's words in its own special language, shuddering delicately beneath his hands, her breasts swelling and firming, her nipples clearly visible beneath the fine fabric of her dress, her eyes suddenly dark and heavy with her emotions as she stared up into the unreadable intensity of his.

'Sweet, loving Alice… How much you have tormented and tantalised me these last few weeks. The scent of your perfume in this room, the sound of your laughter when you are playing with Angelina, the shape of your body beneath your clothes when you move, and my memories of just how it looks without those clothes.

'I want you, Alice! I want to lose myself in your sweetness…forget the pain and the guilt and…'

Alice didn't know which of them it was who shuddered so deeply that both their bodies felt the sensation and she didn't even think she cared. Right now all that mattered was that Marco wanted her; that he needed her and everything that was her welled up inside her to meet that need.

Instinctively she moved closer to him, lifting her mouth generously to his.

He covered it immediately with his own, making her tremble. His kiss was hard and possessive. The kiss of a man driven by fierce passions, she recognised instinctively as he parted the softness of her lips with the swift thrust of his tongue.

His hands were cupping her face, holding her still beneath the elemental possession of his kiss. She could have broken away if she wanted to, Alice knew, but it was as though some force stronger than any desire she might have had to protect herself kept her where she was, her body just brushing against Marco's as slowly, breath by breath, he deepened his kiss.

She felt one of his hands slide from her jaw to her throat, slowly caressing her skin before moving down over her back to rest just below her waist, and then tighten around her so that now she was totally body to body with him.

'Can you feel how much I want you?' he whispered against her ear.

Alice shivered convulsively, her physical reaction betraying just how aware of his arousal she was—aware of it and aroused herself by it.

'You have the most beautiful breasts, just made to be kissed,' he told her thickly. 'What is it? Don't you believe me?' he asked her when she automatically started to shake her head, overwhelmed by the intimacy of what he was saying to her. 'Do you want me to prove to you just how beautiful I think they are?'

The dress Alice was wearing was an old favourite, a slip of black jersey that moved fluidly with her body and that zipped up the back. She tensed a little as she felt Marco reach for the zip, but, even though her eyes widened and filled with uncertainty, her body still trembled with excitement and desire as he unfastened the dress, and slowly slipped it from her shoulders. As it slid to the floor, Alice automatically closed her eyes, afraid not just of her own nakedness but also of what Marco might see in her eyes, the helpless, foolish, aching love she knew might be revealed there.

What she was doing was so reckless. So dangerous, so potentially self-destructive. She knew how he felt about her, or rather how he didn't! Did she really want to burden herself with the knowledge that she was using his present vulnerability to satisfy her own aching longing for him?

She felt him kissing the base of her throat whilst his hands cupped the balls of her shoulders.

The evening air felt softly cool against her naked skin, but Alice knew that it wasn't the air that was making her nipples peak so urgently.

Marco's hands were cupping her breasts, whilst his lips feathered tiny kisses against her closed eyes. She could feel her nipples pressing into the palms of his hands, aching with longing as he slowly caressed her breasts.

Tonight, just as she had been on the night of their wedding, all she had been wearing beneath her dress was a pair of briefs.

'Your skin is so soft. So tenderly pale,' Marco murmured. 'There is something about you, sweet Alice, that brings out the hunter in me, the desire to feast myself on the tender sweetness of your flesh, so very, very different from my own. Does it shock you to hear me say these things to you?' he asked her.

Alice couldn't speak, but had she been able to do so she would have told him that she suspected that he would not be saying them to her if it weren't for the combination of his grief for his dead cousin and the effect of the wine he had drunk. She sensed that together they had lifted the taut control he had been exercising over himself, allowing her to see once more the man who had filled her with such physical pleasure and satisfaction on the night of their wedding. He had wanted her then, and he wanted her again now. Wanted her, yes, but he did not love her, she tried to warn herself.

Her body, though, didn't want to hear her warnings; recklessly it was responding to Marco's touch with flagrant sensuality.

'Don't look at me like that,' he suddenly said thickly as his hand left her breast to cup the back of her neck. Instinctively she looked up at him and then wished she hadn't as she saw the blazing look of desire burning in his eyes.

'Not unless you mean what those huge eyes of yours are saying to me! Do you?' he asked her. 'Do you want me to take you to my bed, and keep you there, sweet Alice, to cover your nakedness with my own and touch you in all the ways that a lover touches a woman, pleasures her. Loves her.'

Alice was shaking so much she suspected that if he hadn't been holding her she wouldn't have been able to stand upright.

He was seducing her with his words just as thoroughly as he was with the slow, seductive caress of his hands on her virtually naked body. Soft, stroking caresses that warmed her flesh and tormented it, making her ache for more, so much, much more...

'You haven't answered me,' he reminded her, bending his head to place a soft kiss at either side of her mouth and then to circle her lips with the tip of his tongue, causing her to melt helplessly against him, her lips parting eagerly for the deep thrust of his tongue.

Instinctively she moved urgently against him, her hands clinging to the fabric of his shirt whilst deep within her body she felt the sharply piercing ache of her own need. Helplessly she returned his kiss with all the intensity burning inside her.

'But now you have,' Marco told her softly as he released her mouth, and swung her up into his arms to carry her over to the bed.

'Now you have told me that you want me as much as I want you.'

As he lowered her onto the bed he placed his lips against her breast, gently caressing her nipple.

Alice gasped and tensed, her whole body a bow of shocked delight as she trembled from head to foot with the intensity of her own pleasure.

That Marco knew what he was doing to her, how he was making her feel, was obvious by the way his own passion suddenly flared into hot, reciprocal hunger, his hand supporting her arched body whilst his mouth caressed her other breast, and not gently this time either, but Alice had gone beyond wanting gentleness. As her body responded to his passion she tried to silence the sharp, high cry of frantic need that rose in her throat and failed, but the sound she had made, so shocking to her, only seemed to incite Marco.

He caressed her breasts with his hands and his mouth until Alice felt she couldn't bear the pleasure any more. It stimulated and excited her, but at the same time it left her feeling empty, aching... Needing.

Frantically she gave in to her own need to respond, pressing small, moist kisses on Marco's throat, his exposed shoulder, where she realised she must have pulled so hard at his shirt she had torn off the button. She could hear the small keening noises she was making as she tried to articulate her need to have the same access to his naked body that he had to hers, but she hadn't realised she had actually stated that need out loud until Marco suddenly released her and sat up beside her, his gaze holding hers, his eyes brilliant with a mixture of male triumph and hot desire as he boldly finished quickly removing his shirt.

'Is this what you want?' he asked her thickly.

Alice couldn't help herself. Immediately she reached out and touched him, her eyes wide and dark. Totally engrossed in what she was doing, in the feel of the soft, silky dark hairs beneath her fingertips, the hot, male scent of his skin, and the way it felt and tasted beneath her lips as she placed them against it, she was oblivious to the fact that Marco was removing the rest of his clothes until the fingers she was blindly smoothing over the tautness of his muscles suddenly dipped low enough to touch the flat plane of his belly.

Immediately she froze, but it was too late, Marco was

urging her to touch him even more intimately, to touch and caress him in the same way, he whispered to her, as he was going to touch and caress her.

As he spoke he was gently teasing her briefs away from her body, his lips feathering delicate kisses against her skin.

'Do you know just what it does to me to know that I have awakened you to your desire, Alice?' he asked her rawly. 'The night of our wedding I hurt you, I know, but I think I gave you pleasure as well. Tell me,' he demanded. 'Tell me if I did?'

Alice moaned. Just listening to what he was saying to her was driving her need to a fever-pitch. Just remembering how she had felt that night...

Her body ached with need for him; it filled every single cell, every nerve ending, the feeling so intense that it was almost a physical pain.

'Tell me,' he was insisting.

Dizzily she thought that it must be a male pride thing that was making him so insistent, unaware of just how much his love for her made him ache to feel that she had some pleasure from his touch.

'It was...it was good,' she admitted unsteadily.

'Good,' Marco repeated. 'How good? So good that you will take the memory of its pleasure with you to the grave? Because if not, tonight it will be that good,' he promised her softly. 'Tonight I will give you all the pleasure there is. All the pleasure you need. Tonight you and I will celebrate life together.'

Alice knew he was thinking about his cousin and the shortness of his life.

Blindly, her own emotions acutely sensitive, she opened her mouth to his kiss.

'I want this to be as good for you as I know it's going to be for me.' She could hear Marco whispering to her, between the deep kisses he was giving her, taking her mouth with possessive passion as his touch became more and more intimate and her body relaxed against it and then began to clamour eagerly for it.

As she arched her hips and writhed helplessly against his hand Alice felt him lift his mouth from hers and groan against her throat whilst his body was convulsed by a long, deep shudder.

Just the feel of his body against hers was making her ache so much with longing for him. There was a need deep inside her, an emptiness that only he could fill, an urgency driving her, compelling her.

When Marco reached for her, Alice wrapped herself around him, her hands clinging to his shoulders, her legs wrapped high and tight around his body, welcoming the remembered sweet, fierce shock of his now careful thrust within her.

Her body seemed to have been made especially for this, especially for him, Alice thought dizzily as every sensitised nerve ending reacted to the feel of him thrusting deeper inside her, in a surge of hot, sweet, wet pleasure that defied description. She had thought it would be impossible for her to feel more pleasure than she had done that first time, but now she knew she had been wrong! That the feeling of being totally filled by him was one that she was enjoying as much as she could sense that he was; that the need that drove him was exactly the same need that drove her to have him there as deep within her as it was possible for him to be, and, once there, to move in exactly the way he was doing, all male, savage, powerful heat and possession, all wonderful, loving pleasure.

Alice gasped as the contractions of her own fulfilment gripped her, more intense, more shocking, more everything that she had ever imagined they might be. She knew she cried out Marco's name and that he responded with a guttural sound of raw, male, agonised release of his own, but these were peripheral recognitions, her whole world, her whole being concentrated on the intimate intensity of the pleasure Marco had just shown her.

As she finally slid down from the heights tears glistened on her cheeks, her eyes dazed and luminous with the intensity of her experience.

Too exhausted to conceal them from him she simply lay there as he brushed them away. It would be so easy now to convince herself that she could see tenderness in his eyes, but she had to remember the realities of her situation. Just because Marco had made love to her, that did not mean that he loved her. He had felt vulnerable. He had needed someone and she had been there.

It would be extremely foolish of her to start imagining anything else.

Marco woke up with a jolt. The bedroom was in darkness, and there was absolutely no sound from the dressing room, which would have indicated that a wakeful Angelina had brought him out of his deep sleep. There was one unfamiliar sound in his room, though, in his bed. There was the soft whisper of Alice's breathing.

Alice! His heart missed a beat and then another before thudding heavily against his chest wall.

The wine he had drunk earlier was no longer intoxicating his bloodstream, and the sharpness of his grief for Aldo had softened to a dull ache, but neither of them was any real excuse for what he had done.

What had happened to the self-control he had always prided himself on having?

The last thing that Alice would want when she woke up, he told himself bitterly, was to find him in bed with her, a reminder of the way he had played on her compassion.

Very carefully Marco slid out of the bed, pausing only to equally carefully and gently tuck the covers protectively around Alice's sleeping body before straightening up. She looked so young, so tender, so desirable in her sleep. Unable to stop himself, Marco leaned down again and tenderly brushed a soft kiss against her lips before heading for the dressing room, and the small narrow bed in there in which Alice normally slept.

When Alice woke up Marco had already left for Rome. Alice told herself that she was glad and that she needed some breathing space without him to give her the strength to cope with her love for him.

She couldn't go on like this. But she couldn't leave either. Just as Marco was doing, she was committed to putting Angelina's needs before her own.

It was nearly a week since Alice had last seen Marco. He had rung her every day and sometimes twice a day during his absence, but only of course to check on Angelina. Tonight he would be home, although he'd informed Alice his flight was not due to arrive until the early hours as he had a final appointment in Rome that would last until after dinner.

The phone rang as she was crossing the salon on her way to the garden with Angelina.

Automatically she answered it, her stomach muscles clenching in nervous excitement as she anticipated hearing Marco's voice, but instead she discovered that her caller was Francine, Angelina's grandmother.

Immediately Francine demanded to speak to Marco.

'I'm afraid that isn't possible,' Alice told her as politely as she could. 'He's away on business at the moment.'

'Oh, it's you!' Francine responded unpleasantly. 'The little nanny, or, should I say, the new *contessa*... Don't think I haven't guessed just what this marriage is all about! Well, he isn't going to get away with it. He isn't going to stop me... I've taken legal advice... When will he be back? I want to see him,' she demanded abruptly.

'Er...'

When Alice hesitated, anxiously, not sure what kind of response Marco would want her to make, but knowing full well just what she would like to say to Francine given free choice, especially about her neglect of her granddaughter, Francine cut across her uncertainty with a contemptuous, 'Trying to protect him? How pathetic! I suppose you've fallen for him…you know he's just using you, don't you? I have every right to see my granddaughter and that is exactly what I intend to do. As of now…and if need be I shall remain at the *palazzo* until Marco does return…'

Alice's heart sank deeper with every word the other woman uttered, but she knew that there was nothing she could say that would prevent her from arriving at the *palazzo*. She just hoped that Marco would return before she did!

For the rest of the day Alice worried anxiously over Francine's threats.

Alice hadn't been sleeping properly since Marco had been away, with the result that by the time she had finished her evening meal she was already yawning.

There was no reason for her not to have an early night, she told herself. Marco was not due back until the early hours, and once he did return there was no reason why he should want to see her, was there?

Some women experienced tiredness in the early weeks of their pregnancy. Alice's heart gave a dizzying thump. By rights she ought to be praying that she was not pregnant, instead of secretly hoping that she was! Marco's baby! Was it wrong of her to long to have his child?

He had sworn that if she did conceive that he would not let him or her go! He had told her too that he knew she would never leave her baby, which meant… She couldn't spend the rest of her life living with him, loving him, knowing that he did not love her! But neither she suspected would she be able to find the strength to leave.

During Marco's absence she had taken to sleeping in the big bed in the main bedroom, not because it was any more comfortable than the smaller bed in the dressing room, but simply, she acknowledged guiltily, because it was Marco's bed. Because being there somehow eased the ache of longing for him that tormented her.

Tonight, though, she would be sleeping in her own bed!

Knowing that he would be arriving home so late, Marco had left his car at the airport. As he drove into the long private drive that led to the *palazzo* he acknowledged both how tired he was and how much he had missed Alice.

In Rome he had constantly been subconsciously looking for her, listening for her laughter, and the sound of her voice, low and loving as she spoke to Angelina.

If she should conceive his child, she would have to stay with him. Just the thought of watching her body grow with his child filled him with a gut-wrenching surge of raw longing. He must not allow himself to think so! Alice had a right to give her love as freely to the man of her choice as he had given his to her! If he tried to deny her that right, then he couldn't love her!

Alice shivered as she remembered her nightmare. In it Francine had been laughing as she'd told them that the courts had decided that Angelina should live with her. Alice's mouth felt dry, and her eyes gritty. Sliding out of her bed, she padded into the main bedroom through which she had to walk to reach the bathroom, and then stopped as the moonlight revealed Marco's sleeping form in the bed in front of her.

He was back! She hadn't even heard him arrive.

Impulsively she tiptoed across to the bed, unable to resist the temptation to look down into his sleeping face. In sleep his features looked gentler, his dark hair tousled, and the beginnings of a beard shadowing his jaw. Without thinking what she was doing, Alice reached out and touched it with her fingertips, wondering dizzily at the sensation of it against her own soft flesh. Even when he was asleep his maleness was a powerful aura that enraptured and held her. Her fingertips had reached his mouth. She started to tremble as she traced the shape of his lips. He was breathing deeply and softly.

She gave a shocked gasp as suddenly his eyes opened at exactly the same time as his mouth closed round her fingertips, and his hands fastened on her waist, jerking her onto the bed beside him.

'Marco,' she protested, but the sensation within her caused by the sensual way he was licking and sucking her fingers made the sound of his name more of a long, shaky moan of desire than any real, recognisable objection.

Her fingertips were released, but her hand was still held captive.

'There's no way I should be doing this,' he groaned. 'And no way that I can stop.'

And then he was kissing her properly, his mouth hungrily demanding on hers.

A fierce surge of pleasure filled her, knowing that he wanted her so much, a dangerous ache filling her womb this time, her body was so eagerly ready—so hungry for his touch that her own lips were parting, her tongue tangling sensually with his the moment she felt his mouth open.

The touch of his hands on her body was every pleasure she could ever want; he was all the pleasure she would ever want, and she couldn't stop herself from showing him how she felt as she pressed tiny, hungry kisses against his throat, his chest, his arms, whilst he pulled her even closer into him. She wanted all of him! Everything! Every sensation, every sense fulfilled and satisfied simply because it was with Marco.

She wasn't a novice bride now. Her body knew him, and it knew itself as well, it knew what desire and pleasure were and how to give and receive them. And he had shown her and taught her all of that, so he had no one but himself to blame, she reasoned passionately.

This time it was his turn to shudder and groan as her

passion surprised and overwhelmed him, her hands revelling in the sensation of touching him, the freedom to touch him wherever she wished, to learn and know him and to feel his response to her, against her hands, against her lips, within her body... She was possessed by a sense of urgency and fate, an inner knowledge, a need to seize this special moment.

To have him, most of all, deep, deep within her, where she wanted to hold him for eternity, whilst she revelled in the female triumph of having given him his pleasure in the same heartbeat as she had taken from him the seeds of eternity. As he spilled himself inside her, Marco cried out in desperation. This was not how it should be, not how he had intended it to be, but somehow he was powerless to deny himself! He started to reach for her, needing to hold her and then realised what he had done.

As Marco moved deliberately away from her, Alice was bitterly aware of his rejection.

CHAPTER TWELVE

'FOR the last time, Francine, no. There is no way I am going to pay you anything—for any reason…'

As he faced Francine's furious disbelief, watching as she paced the floor of the *palazzo*'s library, Marco acknowledged that he was tempted to give in and pay her what she wanted. If he had thought for one minute that in doing so he would remove her from Angelina's life for ever, he would willing have paid three times the amount she was asking him for, but he knew what would happen if he did.

Blackmail was an invidious, creeping thing. Sooner or later and probably sooner, Francine would be back for more money, and if he paid her off now all he would be doing would be creating a situation where she continued to demand blood money from him. If that happened Angelina would never be safe. No, risky though it was, going to court to establish who Angelina should be with was in Marco's opinion the right course of action to take.

'You'll regret this,' Francine warned him bitterly. 'You claim you love Angelina, and yet you won't even part with a measly million dollars to keep her,' she taunted him. 'Some love…'

'I could say the same thing to you,' Marco pointed out coldly to her, 'but then we both know, don't we, Francine, that where you are concerned love doesn't come into the equation, other than your own love for yourself? Has it occurred to you the damage you're doing to your own case by coming here like this and trying to blackmail me?'

'How are you going to prove it?' Francine sneered. 'By producing one of your paid lackeys. My brief will make sure everyone knows that they are dependent on you for everything, and that your word is law here, Marco. And if you're thinking of your new wife…' Her sneer deepened. 'How much did you pay her to marry you? Or did she do it for free? Silly girl…a man always values so much more what he has to pay for. And the more he pays, the more he values it.'

'As I'm sure you have good cause to know, Francine,' Marco responded quietly. 'But if you ever dare again to mention Alice in the same breath as your own sordid set of values, let me warn you right now, I will make sure that you have good cause to regret it.'

'Don't you dare threaten me,' Francine warned him furiously. 'This is your last chance, Marco. If you don't take it, then I promise you I am going to take Angelina away from you. She is my flesh and blood; I am her closest living relative.'

'A mother who sold her own daughter to the highest bidder. No court in the world will give you so much as access to her once they know your history, Francine,' Marco told her coolly, with a confidence he was inwardly fighting to hold onto.

'You'll pay for this, Marco,' Francine threw at him as she turned on her heel. 'My God, I promise you, you are going to wish you had paid me when you had the opportunity because there's no way now I will ever let you have Angelina.'

'That decision doesn't rest with you,' Marco reminded her. However, as he watched her storm out of the *palazzo* and head for her car Marco knew that inwardly he was not as confident as he had pretended.

In a fair and just world he would gain custody of Angelina for her own sake, but…but Francine could be extremely plausible when she chose, and she was also both dangerous and manipulative.

Francine was shaking with fury as she drove away from the *palazzo*. She had been so sure that Marco would give in to her this time. She was desperate for the money she had asked him for…more desperate than he could possibly imagine. There was a dark and dangerous side to Francine's life that not even Patti had known about.

She had first visited the United States as a young woman searching for the GI father who had abandoned her mother without knowing she was pregnant. When she had finally found him Francine had been disappointed to discover that he was far from being the wealthy, successful man she had fantasised about him being, but was in fact a careworn accountant working in a factory in New Jersey.

He had been married with three children, Francine's younger half siblings…whom Francine had liked even less than she had liked her father, but there had been one thing he had done for her and that had been to give her her American nationality.

And it was because of that that she was in so much trouble now. Or at least that was how she perceived her situation.

She had started gambling when she had left her newly discovered father and made her way to Nevada, initially to work as a croupier and then more latterly to spend her earnings at the gaming tables.

It had been there that she had first met Jack. The man who for many years had been her lover, even while Francine had been married and living in England with her husband and Patti. Jack, it was rumoured, had connections with the Mafia. He had loaned Francine money, which over the years had built up into an horrendous amount; an amount that he was now demanding that she repay…either in cash or in another way—helping him with his illegal activities. And it was that other way that had sent Francine into a frantic frenzy to Marco, desperate to get from him the money to repay Jack.

Once she was dragged into his gangster lifestyle, she would never be able to break free. Her punishment if she were to be caught could mean that she might even lose her own American citizenship, and there was no way she wanted that to happen!

The wheels of her hire car spun on the gravel of the *palazzo*'s long driveway.

Alice, who had been walking Angelina in her stroller, saw the cloud of dust thrown up by the speed at which Francine was travelling.

She had been outside in the garden when she had seen the other woman arrive, and she was relieved to see that she was now leaving.

There had to be some way to make Marco pay her that money, Francine fumed frantically. She had been so sure that he would buy her off! That was the whole reason she had threatened to lay claim to Angelina. The last thing she wanted was a dependent child; she had never wanted Patti to have her and had counselled her daughter to have a termination. Marco, of course, being typically Italian, was besotted with the wretched child.

Francine's hands tightened on the steering wheel of the car as she saw Alice with the stroller... With a sudden flash of inspiration she knew that her prayers had been answered, and what she must do.

Pressing her foot to the car's brake, she brought it to a skidding halt.

Alice coughed on the dust Francine's screeching halt had thrown up, wafting it away with her hand, whilst she watched uneasily as Francine got out of the car and walked towards her.

'Give me my grandchild,' Francine demanded imperiously the moment she reached them, stationing herself strategically in front of Alice and reaching swiftly into the stroller, lifting Angelina out before Alice could stop her.

At being handled by a stranger whose touch lacked the loving tenderness she was used to, Angelina immediately started to cry, her distress adding to Alice's anxiety.

'You're frightening her,' she cautioned Francine protectively. 'She isn't used to being held like that. Look let me show you what she likes…'

'I don't give a damn what she does or doesn't like,' Francine retorted unpleasantly, breaking off to give a small angry scream and quickly hold Angelina at arm's length as the baby reacted to her roughness by sicking up some of her food. 'Don't you dare be sick on me, you little brat,' Francine told her furiously, shaking her so hard that Alice immediately tried to remonstrate with her.

'You don't like what I'm doing. Tough!' Francine told Alice contemptuously. 'She's my grandchild and she's coming with me.'

Alice couldn't believe what she was hearing… Francine couldn't possibly just walk off with Angelina like that. Francine was now turning round, still holding Angelina, without any concern for the baby's comfort, and heading for the car, opening the driver's door, and for the first time Alice realised that the engine was still running.

Panic filled her. One read about such things—children being abducted in custody wars—but she had never for one second imagined that it might happen to Angelina.

'You can't take her! Please…' she protested, her throat dry and raw with fear. 'She's just a baby! She doesn't know you… In half an hour she'll need a feed and…'

Frowningly Francine hesitated. What Alice was saying was true! She thought quickly, her eyes narrowing with concentration, and then told Alice, 'Well, if you're so concerned about her, you'd better get in the car as well. Who knows? Perhaps Marco will be prepared to pay double to get the pair of you back!'

Alice stared at her. Francine was kidnapping Angelina in order to make Marco pay to get her back? Frantically she searched the other woman's face. Everything she could see there confirmed all that Alice felt about her, and her fears for Angelina grew.

Francine was carelessly bundling Angelina into the back of her car, which didn't even have a baby seat—in another few seconds she would be gone. It would take Alice at least twenty minutes to get back to the house even if she ran, and by that time…

'Wait!' Alice demanded as Francine started to get into the car, ignoring Angelina's wails of protest. 'I'm coming with you. But we need to take the stroller…it turns into a car seat and—'

'No way! Either get in now or I'll leave,' Francine told her grimly.

What real options did she have? Alice asked herself. None! Shakily she got into the back of the car and tried to comfort Angelina as Francine proceeded to drive off at such a high speed that Alice was jolted back against the seat so heavily that the movement jarred her neck. Thank heavens she had Angelina wrapped protectively in her arms.

'Please,' she begged Francine. 'You are driving much too fast.'

'Poor little wifey. What are you trying to do? Make me slow down so that your wonderful macho husband can catch up with us? No way!' Francine laughed. 'No way do I stop until we're back in Rome and then, my dear, Angelina and I will be on the first flight to the USA where we will stay until your precious husband comes to his senses.'

Alice winced as she was thrown against the car door when Francine turned out of the drive and onto the main road.

There was no way Angelina could endure being driven even a few miles at such a break-neck speed without being sick, never mind all the way to Rome, and thanks to Francine all the baby had was the clothes she was wearing.

Alice had never in the whole of her life hated anyone as much as she loathed and detested Francine. How could she do this to any child, never mind her own grandchild? But Alice already knew there was no point in trying to reason with her. Angelina was snuggling as close as she

could to Alice, her baby eyes round with shock and distress.

'It's all right, little one,' Alice whispered tenderly to her.
'Don't worry…don't worry.'

As she rocked her Alice wished there were someone
there to tell her not to worry… Someone? Or Marco?

Out of the corner of her eye she watched in horrified
disbelief as Francine took a corner by driving in the middle
of the road, and only just missed being hit by the car coming the other way.

'Typical male driver!' Alice heard her mutter as she
increased her speed.

'God, I hate men! All of them, but none of them as
much as I hate your husband,' she told Alice bitterly. 'All
he had to do was to part with a mere million dollars. That
was all. He could have kept the bloody brat and you as
well, but, no…he claims to love the pair of you but he
obviously doesn't love you very much, does he?'

It was news to Alice that Marco had ever claimed to
love her, but wisely she kept her thoughts to herself.
Francine was already dangerously overwrought and frantically Alice tried to think of some way to calm her down
and get her to reduce her speed. If she didn't Alice was
desperately afraid that there could be an accident…

It was half an hour after Francine had driven off with
Angelina and Alice before Pietro, returning from the fields,
saw the abandoned stroller in the drive and rushed to report
what he had seen to Marco.

Marco, who had assumed that Alice was punishing him
for the previous night by keeping away from him, quickly
checked the bedroom and, on finding it empty, immediately hurried to his own car and drove to where Pietro had
found the stroller.

The tyre marks in the gravel told him everything he
needed to know. Francine! Francine was somehow respon-

sible for the abandoned stroller and the disappearance of both Alice and Angelina...

'Oh, my God,' he whispered to himself as he guessed what must have happened. 'Oh, my God!'

Once she got to Rome she would ring Marco from the airport. Just before she boarded her flight, Francine decided gleefully. And she would tell him that now the cost of getting custody of Angelina had doubled to two million dollars, with of course a further million thrown in for the safe return of his wife.

Quite how she was going to persuade Alice to board the plane with her, Francine hadn't worked out as yet, but she suspected that wherever she took Angelina, Alice would follow.

Surely Francine wouldn't simply be able to leave the country with Angelina, Alice fretted.

There would be legalities; formalities; the small matter of a passport, but she hesitated to say anything in case it drove Francine into an even greater frenzy than she was already in.

Angelina had been sick so often as they'd been thrown around the back of the small car that the poor little thing probably didn't have anything left in her tummy to be sick with, Alice recognised as she tried her best to comfort her.

The road from the *palazzo* was a narrow, twisting one as Alice had good cause to know. Even when Marco was driving she sometimes felt nervous, and Marco was a very careful driver.

Francine, on the other hand, was anything but, and Alice could have sworn that sometimes Francine forgot which side of the road she was actually supposed to be driving on!

The inevitable happened just when Alice had finally begun to relax and convince herself that Francine's driving was no worse than that of the drivers coming the other way. She had taken a corner far too fast, and had to swerve to avoid crashing head-on with the lorry coming the other way.

Alice felt the sickening lurch of the car as Francine lost control of it and looked up just in time to realise that they were skidding across the road right in the path of an on-coming car.

Reaching instinctively, she threw herself protectively on top of Angelina whilst the world turned into a hell of twisting, screeching, tearing metal, punctuated by a woman's screams and a series of bone-jarring thuds. She felt the pain in her legs, and then the numbness, but by then a blessed silence had fallen, a stillness in which she was at peace to let go of the pain tearing into her. Just as long as she didn't let go of Angelina...

Later Alice realised it could only have been a matter of minutes after the crash and her loss of consciousness before willing hands were pulling open the doors of the car, calling out to her in anxious voices that dragged her back from the abyss of her agonising pain.

'The baby! You must take the baby!' she heard herself insisting as she managed to twist her head to look into the eyes of the man bending anxiously over her.

Her back had stopped hurting now. She couldn't feel it at all, thank goodness. But she could smell petrol and sense the fear and anxiety of the men clustered around the doorway.

Her thoughts felt muddled and slow; she couldn't see Francine but she could feel Angelina's warm, squirming body lying protectively beneath her own.

'The baby!' she repeated to her would-be rescuers. It was an effort for her to talk, her lips felt numb, but she couldn't lift her hand to touch them because it felt as if the whole of her upper body was trapped beneath some heavy, crushing weight...

'Quick. There is a child in here,' she heard one of the

men say in Italian. And then another called out, 'We shall need to cut the woman free!'

Cut the woman free. What woman? Who were they talking about? Francine? Even though she disliked her, Alice hoped that she would be all right…

'The baby,' she repeated painfully…as the man leaning over her started to fade and recede in a sickening wave of dizziness… Angelina had managed to free one of her arms, and she reached out and touched Alice's face.

Alice could see the shock in the man's face, which irrationally annoyed her. Hadn't he listened to anything she had said?

'You must tell Marco, the *conte*, that Angelina is safe,' she told him slowly, as though she were talking to a child. 'He will be worried about her. You must contact the *palazzo*. Slowly and painstakingly she gave him the address and the telephone number, resisting the desire to cling onto Angelina as she was gently eased out from beneath her own body.

They had to hold her whilst someone put a huge wadding of cushions and what looked like discarded clothes beneath her where Angelina had been. Indignantly she tried to protest, but she could feel herself slipping into unconsciousness.

It took Marco less than half an hour after the police had informed him about the accident to reach the scene—he had driven there far faster than Francine, dreading with every kilometre what he'd been going to find.

Angelina, they had told him, was fine.

'And Alice? My wife?'

There had been a brief pause.

'She is trapped in the back of the car. She must have thrown herself over the baby to protect her and the force of the collision has pushed the whole of the passenger seat of the car into the back seat and over her,' he had been told sombrely.

When Marco reached the scene of the accident it was thronged with people.

'Your wife will have to be cut free,' he was told. 'We have had to send to Florence for the cutting gear...'

His heart buckled and twisted, tearing him apart. He had to be with Alice and nothing, no one was going to stop him.

'I must go to my wife,' he told the policeman grimly.

Even saying the simple words 'my wife' agonised him, bringing home to him just how much Alice meant to him, and how much he loved and needed her.

'She is unconscious at the moment.' The policeman frowned. 'There has been a spillage of fuel caused by the collision. And it isn't safe to allow anyone to get too close.'

Handing Angelina to Maddalena, whom he had brought with him, Marco demanded quietly, 'Let me see.'

Without waiting for the policeman's response, Marco pushed his way through the police cordon surrounding the accident and then stopped, his head spinning.

This was worse than the accident that had killed Aldo and Patti. The small car had virtually been crushed to nothing by the force of the impact with the much heavier vehicle it had skidded into. Ironically the driver's side of the vehicle was intact, but the passenger side...

'It is a miracle that your daughter is unhurt,' the policeman told Marco. 'Mother love is a wonderful thing. Your wife risked her own life to save her baby. She threw herself over the baby and her body protected her. Unfortunately—' gravely he looked at Marco '—unfortunately, she is now trapped beneath the front of the car and the passenger seat. We cannot move her, and we do not know just how badly hurt she is. The doctor has just arrived and he is trying to talk to her.'

His heart in his mouth, Marco strode over to the car. A man was crouched down beside the open passenger door, stroking Alice's hand.

'Can you feel anything…any pain—any sensation?' he was asking her quietly.

Alice was trying to concentrate on what she was being asked, but it was so very, very difficult! All she wanted to do was to close her eyes and go to sleep. Her body felt odd…heavy and yet somehow numb. There was a dreadful pain in her head and a metallic taste in her mouth. Her hand looked unfamiliar to her…limp and odd… At least Angelina was safe, she comforted herself hazily.

'No, you must stay awake,' the doctor was saying sternly to her. 'Don't close your eyes.'

Alice winced as he flicked his fingers painfully on the back of her hand. He was turning his head to speak to someone out of her line of vision, and she couldn't hear what he was saying.

Panic and fear swept through her as she tried to listen. She felt so alone!

An even greater depth of fear was surging through Marco as he reached the doctor and demanded to know what was happening.

'It is important that she remains conscious,' the doctor informed Marco, who had heard Alice's small gasp of fear and was reaching out protectively towards her.

'We don't know just what damage may have been caused as yet…and we won't know until we can cut her free. I shall need to stay here with her and talk to her. Keep her conscious,' the doctor explained patiently to Marco, recognising his feelings.

'Let me do that,' Marco demanded immediately. 'She is my wife.'

The doctor was frowning, but Marco was insistent.

Alice could hear Marco speaking to her; calling her name. Telling her that she must not go to sleep.

Hazily she tried to focus on his voice. How could he possibly be here?

Disbelievingly she forced her heavy eyelids to lift, her eyes widening in shock as she saw that she had not been imagining him, dreaming foolish dreams, he was here. Marco was here with her!

Joy filled her in an adrenalin, life-giving surge, quickly followed by guilt as she realised that he could not possibly be here for her, but because of Angelina.

'I tried to stop Francine,' she told him immediately, 'but she had Angelina. She said she was going to make you pay to get her back…'

Tears filled her eyes. And she gave a small gasp as Marco gently started to wipe them away.

There was blood on the cloth in his hand, she realised with a vague sense of shock.

'You must have cut yourself,' she told him in concern.

'It's nothing,' Marco told her. His voice sounded rough, as though something was stuck in his throat, as though he was somehow having trouble speaking. Because he was angry? With her?

Unaware of what Alice was thinking, Marco dipped his head so that Alice wouldn't see the tears in his eyes. The blood was hers from the cuts on her face, which the doctor had insisted were only superficial, but he didn't want to frighten her by telling her that.

It was hot inside the car, and his muscles were already aching from the crouched position he had adopted so that he could get as close to her as he could. Holding her free hand in his whilst he talked to her, telling her how brave she had been, reassuring her that Angelina was safe.

Alice felt as though she were in some kind of dream, lying there with Marco beside her, holding her hand tightly, smoothing the hair back off her face with his hand whilst he talked to her.

'How do you feel?' he was asking her. 'Are you in any pain?'

'My back really hurt when it first happened,' Alice told him confidingly, 'but the pain's gone now.'

'Has it? That's good,' Marco responded, whilst inwardly he made himself a vow that, no matter how badly injured she was, he would devote the rest of his life to taking care of her and loving her.

This was all his fault. All of it…

'Where's Francine?' Alice asked him.

'I don't know,' Marco answered her truthfully.

One of the witnesses had stated that they had seen a woman running away from the scene of the accident and he had assumed that she must have been Francine.

The truck with the cutting gear had arrived and the police were warning Marco that for his own safety he would have to move away.

Fiercely he refused.

'What a lot of noise,' Alice whispered as the machines were put to work.

'Mmm… You'll soon be free now,' Marco comforted her.

An ambulance was standing by and he could see the doctor watching and waiting.

From somewhere Alice was bleeding. He could see the red stickiness as they started to move the wreckage away from her.

'It hurts!' Alice whispered shakily. Her face was paper-white, her eyes huge and dazed with pain.

'Try to be brave just a little while longer,' Marco whispered to her, barely able to choke out the words.

The doctor was moving towards them, a hypodermic syringe in his hand…

'This is just going to relax you so that we can move you safely,' he told Alice.

She squeezed Marco's hand tightly as the needle slid into her vein.

*   *   *

'So today you are going home. What a pity,' the nurse teased Alice. 'We are going to miss seeing that handsome husband of yours.'

Alice gave her a brief smile. She had grown so used to her hospital bedroom these last four weeks. Felt so safe there that she felt reluctant to leave.

Everyone had been so kind to her; so protective of her. So ready to reassure her that she was very brave and very lucky.

Her worst injury had been the blood she had lost where the metal had pierced her flesh, but even the scar from that would fade in time, the doctor had assured her jovially.

Mercifully she had been spared any real awareness of those agonising hours when she had first been brought to the hospital and they had had to find out just how badly injured she might have been. Her back had been badly bruised. So badly that she had been black and blue, but by some miracle no permanent damage had been done apart from a small fracture to her collar-bone, which had now healed.

The scratches that had covered her face had also totally healed, and now the doctor had decided that she was well enough to leave. To go home… Home to Angelina and to Marco.

Marco! Was she strong enough to be with him and not betray her feelings to him?

And at least something good had come out of the accident. When the police had caught up with Francine at the airport she had been so terrified that she had willingly agreed to sign a document renouncing any claim on Angelina. As Marco had said to Alice, there was no way any court anywhere would grant her custody once they learned how narrowly she had escaped a prison sentence for dangerous driving and for putting at risk the life of the very child she claimed to love so much.

Tersely Marco had told Alice how much he regretted not simply handing Francine the money she had demanded, but, as Alice had told him, in her opinion all that would have done would have been to convince Francine that she could continue to blackmail him whenever she chose. And then Angelina would never have been safe.

But now Alice was afraid to return to normal life, and afraid too to return to the *palazzo*, because the reality was that now, with the threat of Francine fully removed from Angelina's life, Marco no longer needed her. At least not as a wife. And that meant...

Alice didn't want to think about what it meant.

'Ready, then?'

Nervously Alice nodded, watching as Marco picked her bag up off her bed and turned towards the door of her hospital room. At her own insistence, Alice was holding Angelina. Just as soon as Alice had been well enough she had pleaded with the nurses to allow her to have Angelina with her as much as possible, so that the little girl would not feel that she had abandoned her, which was of course why Marco had visited the hospital so much and stayed overnight—for Angelina's benefit, not for hers.

The one thing Alice had asked Marco to do for her had been not to inform her family about what had happened. Her sister had confided excitedly to her just before the accident that she was pregnant and Alice had not wanted her to worry.

Alice had been dreading the drive back to the *palazzo*, but, to her surprise, instead of driving her himself Marco got into the back of the car with her after he had strapped Angelina into her front baby seat, leaving Pietro to drive.

'It's all right, Alice,' he told her quietly, as though he had guessed how she was feeling. 'You'll be perfectly safe.'

And somehow Alice suddenly felt that she would be. But what surprised her even more than the fact that Marco was travelling in the back of the car with her was the way in which he calmly took hold of her hand and held it firmly within his own.

Alice stiffened as she tried to conceal her shock. Not once in all the time she had been in hospital had Marco ever touched her. In fact, she had gained the impression that he wanted to keep as much physical distance between them as he could, just as he had done at the *palazzo*, when she had known that he'd wanted to underline to her the fact that their sexual intimacy was just that and meant nothing emotional to him.

Just to sit there with her hand folded into the warm protection of his made her ache with emotional weakness. If only she could give her love full rein, and move closer to him, put her head on his shoulder and be drawn protectively into his arms. Desperately afraid that she might somehow betray to him just what her feelings for him were, she pulled her hand from his.

As he felt Alice withdraw her hand from his Marco stared out of the car window. Her rejection of his touch brought home to him the extent of his sins against her. He was facing a choice it was almost impossible for him to make.

On the one hand there was Angelina, who loved and needed Alice so much. Marco hardly dared let himself even begin to quantify the extent of the emotional damage it would do the little girl to lose Alice now. In the first hours of Alice's accident, when Angelina had been of necessity separated from her, she had cried unceasingly, and been inconsolable, until in desperation Marco had taken her to the hospital. The moment he had placed Angelina on the bed with Alice she had calmed down, and incredibly in her semi-conscious state, as though somehow she had known the baby had been there, Alice had reached out and placed her arm protectively around her.

No, Marco knew there could be no substitute in Angelina's life for Alice and Alice's mother love.

But on the other hand, there was Alice. Alice who had suffered so terribly because of him. Alice who surely had the right to love the man of her own choice, and to share his life with him, to bear his children. Marco tensed against the visceral savagery of his own pain at that thought.

What the hell should he do?

Knowing Alice, he suspected that she would insist on honouring her original contract to stay with Angelina for the early years of her life. And if she did, how the hell was he going to find the self-control to keep his distance from her?

Even if they ended their marriage, it wouldn't make any difference; he would still love her, still want her. It was his duty to protect her as it was to protect all those who worked for him—a feudal viewpoint perhaps, but one that was bred into him. But how could he protect her from himself?

Alice tensed as they reached a narrow hairpin bend. She needn't have worried, though; Pietro was a calm and careful driver.

Even so she was relieved when they finally reached the *palazzo*. Relieved and too tired to make any real demur when Marco announced that she was to go straight up to their room so that she could rest.

'They've started work on the new master suite,' he informed her.

'I would have liked to have had it finished in time for your return, but unfortunately that just wasn't possible. Mind you, that is perhaps as well, since I suspect you will want to oversee their decoration and refurbishment yourself. There's a firm I've used before who are experts at providing modern-day fittings such as wardrobes and the like, but fronted in such a way that they blend perfectly into the fabric of older buildings. As soon as you feel strong enough I'll set up a meeting with them, and with the two bathroom specialists whose stuff you liked.'

Alice almost missed one of the stairs. He was still planning to go ahead with the conversion?

Why?

She had had plenty of time to think whilst she had been

in hospital, and she had told herself that, with the threat of Francine permanently removed from Angelina's life, the first thing that Marco would want to do would be to end their marriage.

She had told herself that she ought to be pleased and that, with their marriage over, it would surely be far easier for her to conceal her love from him.

She couldn't possibly leave Angelina, of course, and if Marco should suggest that she did…

Weak tears filled her eyes at the thought of leaving the little girl. They were outside the bedroom door now, and as Marco opened it he told her brusquely, 'I'll leave you to get settled. Maddalena will be up shortly to see if you need anything.'

As he turned away from her Marco caught the silver shimmer of her tears, and stopped.

'What is it?' he demanded immediately. 'Why are you crying? Are you in pain? Where does it hurt? Tell me.'

Alice gave a small hiccupping sob. Trust Marco to think that the pain had a physical cause! But before she could say anything, to her bemusement Marco suddenly burst out, 'Alice. Alice, please don't cry. I can't bear it. I can't bear to think of how much you've suffered. Of how much I have caused you to suffer. I never meant it to happen, I swear to you.'

'No. No. Don't,' Alice heard him begging her as her tears fell even faster in reaction to her shock at realising that somehow he had discovered that she loved him.

'I didn't want it to happen either,' she wept, barely aware of the fact that they were now both inside the bedroom, and Marco was for some reason holding her in his arms.

'I didn't want to love you,' she told him. 'I…'

She could feel the tension in his body. The arms that had been holding her so comfortingly slackened and Marco stepped back from her. Alice shivered, missing their comfort.

'Alice, what are you saying?'

There was a shocked, almost warning note in his voice, but Alice ignored it.

What did it matter what she said now? After all, he had made it obvious that he knew she loved him.

'I'm saying that I love you, Marco. That I'll always love you and that I wish more than anything else in the world that I had conceived your child,' she told him recklessly. 'At least then I'd have something of you, to love. I know you don't want me. I know you'll want to end our business arrangement now, but please, for Angelina's sake, let me stay with her as you originally planned. She needs me, Marco, and I promise that I won't...'

As the words poured out of her Marco could only stare at her in disbelief.

'That you won't what?' he challenged her huskily when he realised that she had stopped speaking.

Alice shook her head, her face crimsoning as she refused to put into words just what she meant.

'That you won't allow me to do this,' Marco suggested, shocking her as he took her back in his arms, and bent his head to feather tiny little kisses against her lips...

'Or this,' he murmured softly against them as his tongue gently probed their closed line and helplessly it started to part.

Alice was shaking with anguish and longing. What was Marco trying to do to her?

Why was he tormenting her like this? And then to her disbelief she heard him telling her thickly, his voice raw with emotion. 'Alice, Alice, my little love, my dearest and only love. I hardly dare let myself believe that this is real. That you should love me when I have done so little to deserve your love.'

Marco was calling her his dearest love. His only love. Dizzily Alice tried to make sense of what was happening, but Marco was kissing her so passionately that it was impossible for her to think!

* * *

Several minutes later, having reluctantly released her mouth, Marco groaned.

'You should be resting…'

But as he looked at her there was a question, a fiery longing in his eyes that made Alice's heart beat very fast, and she couldn't stop the self-conscious colour warming her face as she instinctively looked from Marco to the familiar bed.

'Don't look at me like that,' Marco protested rawly. 'I am only a man, and the fear and despair I have gone through these last weeks!' He paused and shook his head. 'I thought I knew the full pain of loss, but I was wrong. I knew nothing. If I had lost you, my own life would no longer have been worth living.'

Alice fought to drag air into her lungs as her emotions reacted to what he was saying to her.

'But for me you would never have been in that car. If I had paid Francine instead of…'

Alice could hear the guilt in his voice. He had said that he loved her, but was that love merely a by-product of his guilt?

'You don't…you don't have to love me…' she told him, trying to find the right words for her thoughts.

'Yes. I do,' Marco contradicted her immediately. 'I have to love you, Alice, because that is my fate; my destiny… I think I probably knew that within hours of us meeting,' he added wryly.

Alice stared at him.

'Of course, I tried to deceive myself,' Marco continued grimly. 'After all, no man likes to admit that he is no longer in control of his own life. I had assumed that when I chose to marry it would be a calm, rational decision made for logical, sensible reasons. Of course I would respect and care for my wife, and of course…'

'She would not be British, and accused of sleeping around?' Alice supplied ruefully for him.

'You are right to remind me of my misjudgement of you,' Marco acknowledged bleakly. 'It does me no credit, and fills me with shame.'

'I can understand that a man in your position, with your family history, would have traditional values and traditional expectations,' Alice told him quietly, carefully searching for the words she needed. 'The fact that you believed that I was sexually promiscuous—'

'No.' Marco stopped her sharply. 'I admit I tried to think that of you as a means of self-defence, to protect myself from loving you when it seemed that you did not love me, but it didn't take very long in your company, Alice, for me to recognise and be humbled by the true, shining purity of your spirit. And once I had recognised that...' He paused.

'On the day of our wedding when we exchanged our vows, I knew that I loved you, and that I would always love you. I was even foolish enough to feel proud of the fact that my love was so strong and irrefutable. Unfortunately I was not strong enough to control my... feelings.'

There was a huge lump of emotion in Alice's throat. His quiet words meant so much to her.

'Unfortunately,' Marco continued wryly, 'I was not strong enough to control my...feelings, when faced by the temptation of knowing that you....'

'That you believed I was sexually available?' Alice supplied for him.

Immediately Marco shook his head.

'No. Certainly not. That was never in my thoughts,' he denied sternly. 'No, what I was going to say was knowing that you were my wife.'

'But it shocked you to discover that you were my first lover,' Alice reminded him. 'And when you were so distant with me and told me that it must never happen again, I realised you didn't love me.'

'On the contrary, it was very much because I did love you,' Marco corrected her ruefully.

'I had already misjudged you and now I had…abused the trust you had placed in me by agreeing to our marriage. I knew I couldn't trust myself; that I couldn't control myself; that once I touched you I wouldn't be able to stop. That was why I tried to distance myself from you—for your protection. If I had thought for one moment that you returned my love…'

Alice looked at him, her face pink.

'I should have thought that the way I responded to you…in…in bed must have given you some hint!'

'Perhaps it would have done,' Marco agreed, 'if I hadn't already convinced myself that your natural passion and innocence was responsible for the irresistibly sexy way you gave yourself to me. In fact that just gave me another reason to feel guilt and blame. And if you had conceived my child…'

Leaning her face against his chest, Alice whispered softly, 'I so much hoped that I would…'

'Alice…' She felt him shudder as he groaned her name, his arms tightening around her.

'If you had so much as given me a hint that you wanted that…'

A shyly mischievous look lightened Alice's eyes as she lifted her head and looked at him.

'I thought I'd given you much more than a hint,' she teased him gently, remembering how she had wantonly encouraged him to lose himself in her.

'Perhaps I wasn't concentrating,' Marco returned throatily, giving her a look that sent a thrill of pure longing right through her body.

'Perhaps you could hint to me again?'

'What, now?' Alice breathed recklessly.

Now, when there was no need for him to conceal it any more, the blaze of love and desire in his eyes was making her feel as if she were about to melt.

Daringly she reached up to kiss him, shivering with delight as she felt the shuddering reaction of his body to her intimacy. Her mouth brushed his, savouring its familiar shape and taste.

'Alice,' Marco warned her rawly.

Recklessly she ran the tip of her tongue along the outline of his lips, gasping in excited pleasure when his mouth covered hers, capturing her marauding tongue.

'Take me to bed, Marco,' she whispered throatily, when she was finally able to speak.

'Are you sure you're well enough for this?' Marco demanded solicitously a few minutes later as he gently pushed her hair back off her face and looked down at her where she lay against the pillows, her face flushed from the passion of the kisses they had just exchanged.

Her top was unfastened, revealing the creamy line of her throat and the soft swell of her breasts.

One of Marco's hands lay possessively against the full curve of one of them and Alice shuddered in wanton pleasure as he caressed it.

'I think it could be the best form of therapy I could possibly have,' she responded demurely, her own mouth curving into a tender little smile as she reached up to pull him closer to her.

'I don't know what I would have done if I had lost you,' Marco told her emotionally over an hour later as she lay sated and blissfully happy in the curve of his warmth, whilst the afternoon sun streaming in through the window played softly on their naked bodies.

'My life would have been over if you had been killed in that accident, Alice. Promise me you will never, ever doubt again that I love you.'

'I promise,' Alice assured him.

EPILOGUE

Five years later.

'DO YOU know what day it is today?' Marco asked Alice teasingly as he bent his head to kiss her upturned face.

She was in the small special courtyard at the back of the *palazzo* which they had turned into a safe play area for their children, and Marco had just returned from Florence where he had been overseeing some restoration work.

'Of course I do.' She laughed as she returned his kiss.

Out of the corner of her eye she could see their children: their four-year-old son Giancarlo, and the twin daughters who had been born eighteen months ago, and, of course, Alice's secret favourite, Angelina, who was firmly preventing the twins from fighting over their toys.

Like all children, theirs were individual and unique, and that was how she loved them, individually and uniquely, just as she could love the new baby who was due to make his or her arrival in another four months' time, but Angelina would always be extra special to her, just as the bond of love between them was extra special.

When she had risked her own life to protect Angelina's Alice had reacted as a mother, putting her child's safety before her own, and somehow in that split heartbeat of time a bond had been forged between the two of them that was just as strong as the umbilical cord that had bonded her to her birth children. Whenever strangers remarked on how alike she and Angelina were, they always shared knowing special smiles. No mother should have favourites, but sometimes a mother could just not help herself!

186

'So?' Marco demanded. 'What date is it?'

'The date you asked me to marry you,' Alice responded promptly, laughing as she added wickedly, 'For Angelina's sake.'

'For Angelina's sake and for my own sanity,' Marco agreed wryly, releasing her as Angelina left the twins to their own devices and ran across to join them, lovingly cuddling into Alice's side.

'I hope this isn't going to be more twins,' she told Alice feelingly as she patted her growing bump.

Alice laughed. Both she and Marco already knew that the baby she was carrying was another son, but that was going to be their secret.

'I think it's time to take the twins upstairs for their nap,' Alice told Marco ruefully as she hugged Angelina lovingly.

'Mmm,' Marco agreed, watching as Sibilla attempted to hit her twin with the doll she had wrested from her. 'I think I'll come with you.'

'Oh, you two aren't going to get all soppy, are you?' Angelina protested, rolling her eyes in five-year-old disgust.

'Mmm. Sounds like a good idea to me,' Marco murmured to Alice as they watched her run back to join Giancarlo.

'And to me,' Alice agreed softly.

If someone, anyone, had tried to tell her five years ago just how her life was going to turn out she would never have believed them, never have dared to believe she could be so loved or so happy...

But she was, and according to Marco he fully intended to make sure that she remained so for the rest of their lives together!

The world's bestselling romance series.

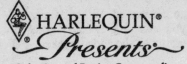

HARLEQUIN®
Presents

Seduction and Passion Guaranteed!

She's his in the bedroom, but he can't buy her love…

The ultimate fantasy becomes a reality in Harlequin Presents®

Live the dream with more *Mistress to a Millionaire* titles by your favorite authors.

MISTRESS TO A MILLIONAIRE

Coming in May

THE ITALIAN'S TROPHY MISTRESS
by Diana Hamilton #2321

Pick up a Harlequin Presents® novel and you will enter a world of spine-tingling passion and provocative, tantalizing romance!

Available wherever Harlequin Books are sold.

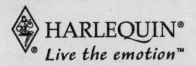

HARLEQUIN®
Live the emotion™

Visit us at www.eHarlequin.com

HPMTAMIL